TO THE MEDICINE BOW

BUCKSKIN CHRONICLES BOOK 5

B.N. RUNDELL

WOLFPACK
PUBLISHING
— EST 2013 —

Published in the United States by Wolfpack Publishing, Las Vegas.

Wolfpack Publishing
6032 Wheat Penny Avenue
Las Vegas, NV 89122

wolfpackpublishing.com

Library of Congress Control Number: 2018908733

Paperback ISBN: 978-1-62918-821-8
eBook ISBN: 978-1-62918-830-0

TO THE MEDICINE BOW

THE SPRING DAYS WERE STRETCHING THEMSELVES out to give the new green shoots ample time to work their way through the tundra of the mountain meadows. Soon the spring greens would color the clearings and join with the myriad of colors of mountain flowers to paint the already beautiful Wind River mountain range. Nestled in the black timber at the edge of a small clearing was the cabin of Caleb and Clancy Mae Thompsett. Still newlyweds by most standards, the young couple had just marked their second anniversary. Their home was the snug little cabin originally built by Jeremiah and Laughing Waters, the adopted parents of the current inhabitants. As Laughing Waters had assumed the responsibility of Shaman for her Arapaho people, it was necessary for her and Jeremiah to move to the village. That move gave the parents ample reason to gift the young couple with their first home, the cabin in the clearing.

This same clearing had been the site of the original

cabin that belonged to Ezekiel, an escaped slave and adopted father of Jeremiah and member of the Arapaho tribe. When a band of slave catchers attacked and killed Ezekiel and burned the cabin, Jeremiah escaped and launched a vengeance quest that took him back East to fulfill a promise to his mentor. Now with a new cabin and a new generation of family, the saga continues. Caleb, known as Talks to the Wind because of his ability to mimic the sounds of many animals, and Clancy Mae, known as Sun of the Morning because of her flaming red hair, were determined to continue the lifestyle they had grown accustomed to as they grew to maturity under the tutelage of their adopted parents. They were suited for this wilderness living with most of their young lives spent in these same woods. Caleb, the step-son of Jeremiah's sister, had come West with Jeremiah at the behest of his dying mother and grew to manhood as the adopted son of Jeremiah, or White Wolf, and Laughing Waters as part of the Arapaho people. Clancy was the sole survivor of a small wagon train done in by a war party of Crow and was rescued by Jeremiah and Caleb and taken in by Jeremiah and Waters as their adopted daughter. Now after growing up together, the unrelated brother and sister were husband and wife, a natural coupling as the only whites among their Arapaho village.

The warm spring days still yielded to cold nights and Caleb and Clancy were cuddled together under the heavy buffalo robe on their bed and sleeping soundly when they were suddenly awakened by the screaming whinny of horses. The accompanying roar that echoed through the clearing told Caleb his horses were under attack by a bear, and a big one by the sound of him. Throwing aside the heavy robe, he hit the floor with his stocking feet and reached to the corner of the room for his Hawken rifle, slipped the powder horn and possibles bag over his head and grabbed the carved door handle. Jerking the door open, the smoldering fire in the fireplace glowed enough to reveal a well-muscled body clad only in a faded red union suit of long underwear with a rear flap only partially closed. His clean-shaven face still bore evidence of his youth but determined eyes and firm set jaw bespoke his maturity. Three long strides brought him to the front door of the cabin, a stealthy peek through the crack showed the danger was twenty yards away at the log corral and lean-to shelter that housed their saddle horses.

Rearing on hind legs with front feet pawing the air, Caleb's spotted rump appaloosa stallion screamed at the standing Grizzly and both animals glared at each other daring their opponent to attack. Old Ephraim, as the big Grizzlies are called by mountain men, was clawing at the top rail seeking access and with every attempt at pulling on a log he roared his defiance and was met with the thundering hooves of the enraged stallion. The glow from the full moon showered the clearing with enough light to show the way to Caleb as his long strides took him closer to the combat. The stench of the bear was a familiar one to the wilderness dweller and told of an old bear that had earned his way to maturity and marked his territory far and wide and bullied his way to the top of the food chain. The cacophony of roars and screaming whinnies vibrated the pines that circled the clearing and echoed off the distant mountain side. Pacing at the back of the corral with a frightened look and wide eyes was the mare of Clancy's that had almost identical markings to Caleb's stallion. The throaty rumble that told of her fear was scarcely heard amidst the argument of the two larger opponents that displayed their belligerence of one another. The stallion seemed to be daring the bear to enter his domain as each attempt of the Grizzly to tear at the log corral was met with an attack of sharp striking hooves. The lightning response of the Grizzly had brought blood to the fore leg of the stallion and as the bear stood to his height of eight feet he cocked his head to the side and with jaws open wide let loose a roar that would curdle the blood of a lesser foe. The roar was suddenly stifled as the Hawken in the hands of Caleb let loose its own roar of assault and spat a .54 caliber ball of lead and belched a cloud of grey white smoke as he launched his attack in defense of his horses. A puff of dust and a small blossom of red marked the entrance point of the ball on the left chest just behind the extended left leg of the mountain of silver-tipped fur standing before him. The bear swiveled on his hind legs to face the new threat, and with another heart stopping roar started a clumsy walk on his hind legs in the direction of the funny looking creature in red underwear. Frozen in place, Caleb slapped his thigh in a natural move to find his missing bowie knife, then dropped the butt of his Hawken to the ground and scratched for his powder horn, pulled the stopper with his teeth and poured powder down the barrel, reached for his possibles bag without taking his eyes off the bear that had dropped to all fours for a charge, he dug for a ball neglecting the thought of a patch, grabbing one he was startled to hear the roar from another Hawken from the direction of the cabin. The big ball from the surprise shot pierced the neck of the bear and with a broken neck the grizzly dropped to skidding halt just three strides from the feet of Caleb. A quick glance at the massive head showed blood coming from the nose and no sign of life. Turning toward the cabin, he saw his very pregnant wife standing in her night shirt with her Hawken to her side and the barrel emitting a thin curl of smoke. The broad smile on her face signaled her relief as she said, "I couldn't let him take you before the baby was born, now could I?"

Shaking his head in wonder at his amazing woman, Caleb trudged back to the cabin with the purpose of getting some clothes on and preparing to take care of the bear carcass. With the horses still nervously pacing the corral, he wasted little time shucking into his buckskins and moccasins, grabbing his Arkansas toothpick, otherwise known as Bowie knife, and returning to the corrals. He fetched his saddle and blanket and halter from the tack shack and made his way to the corral, threw the gear on the top rail, and let himself in with the horses. Talking softly to the horses to reassure them, he reached for the nose of his mount, stroked his head and with the other hand patting his neck he slipped the halter over his head and led him outside the corral to the opposite side from the carcass. He quickly saddled the horse and tethered him to the top rail, slipped the end of the rope around the saddle horn, took the looped end to the carcass and wrapped it around the bear's hind feet. Returning to his appaloosa, he walked beside him as he led the horse now pulling the carcass, to the far side of the cabin to a grassy patch near the edge of the trees. He threw the end of the rope over the large limb of the tall ponderosa, reattached it to the saddle horn and led the horse away from the tree to hoist the carcass off the ground. With so much weight to the bear, the horse had to dig in his hooves and lean into the pull to force the dead weight from the ground. Leading the horse to another nearby tree, Caleb struggled with the task of getting the rope around the tree, snubbed off and released from the horn, but with shear strength, effort and determination, he finally succeeded. He led the horse back to the corral, removed the saddle and let the appaloosa back into the pen to keep his companion mare company and hopefully settle both horses down.

Now the work began. Back at the carcass with the nose and front legs still on the ground, he reached as high as he could and began the long slit from anus to throat to start the removal of the innards. Bears have a natural and unique stench about them from marking their territory to rolling in offal, but when the steam and contents of the stomach cavity were released and multiplied the stench, Caleb trotted away from the task to empty his own stomach behind the trees. Lifting his head and breathing deeply for fresh air, he walked in a wide circle before returning to his task. Using an old ground sheet to catch the innards and excess blood, he would later drag the scraps far away from the cabin because of the smell attracting the many carrion eating predators in the woods.

The silver glow of the moonlit night slowly turned to

the grey sky of early morning as Caleb began the task of skinning the large carcass of the Grizzly. He had already decided to give the meat from the bear to the people of the village but he was keeping the skin for a warm robe and the claws for a necklace and decoration for the buckskin jacket Clancy had been secretly working on as a gift for him. He just had to keep from letting her know he knew about her secret project. As he was finishing, he was joined by Clancy as she encouraged him to come in for some breakfast. "I fixed you some fresh biscuits and elk steak with a couple of sage hen eggs just the way you like," she said with a mischievous smile tugging at the corner of her mouth.

"The way you're lookin' at me, you must have something up your sleeve, what is it?"

"Oh nothin' it just seems like it's gonna be a good day."

"Ummhmmm, when you start lookin' like that, I'm usually in some kind of trouble or else you've got something in store for us, come on, out with it," coerced Caleb.

"We'll see . . ." she tossed over her shoulder as she looked coyly back at him as she made her way back to the cabin.

Sitting at the table, she watched as he hungrily devoured the ample meal she sat before him. Looking down at the food on her plate, she picked at it with a preoccupied expression on her face. Caleb watched as she unconsciously rubbed a hand across the top of her protruding belly and noticed a slight movement that must have been the baby. Looking back at his wife's face, he saw her forehead wrinkle as she tried to hide what he was certain was a pain.

"Are you all right? Is something wrong?" he asked with concern tingeing his voice.

She stretched her back, leaned her head back a little, and with effort said, "I think you need to go get Ma, I think I'm gonna need some help."

"Is it the baby? Is it time? Is he coming now?"

"Not if you don't go get me some help, he won't!"

He helped her up from the chair and to the bed. As she sat on the edge of the bed, she said, "You better get a move on, I think he's in a hurry."

"O.K., O.K., I'll be right back, don't do anything till we get back, ya hear?"

He grabbed the Hawken from the corner of the room and ran from the cabin like the Grizzly was still after him.

THE ENTIRE VILLAGE WAS ALARMED WHEN CALEB rode recklessly through the lodges to come to a sliding stop in front of Laughing Waters teepee. "Ma, Ma, come quick! It's Clancy and she's havin' the baby!" A smiling face framed by long black braids peered from the lodge opening and said, "Well, greetings to you my son, but the way you are acting, one would think this was the first time a child was ever born."

"Yeah, it is! This is the first time for her! Hurry! But you knew . . . "

The giggle from his mother taunted him and he knew he was acting like a crazy man, but this was his first time as a father and he wasn't too sure just how he should be acting. After Waters stood tall, the lodge cover was pushed aside and Jeremiah joined the excited duo with a broad smile stretching his face from under his full beard. He looked down at his wife and said, "Sounds like we're gonna be grandparents."

"Yes it does. Husband, would you please go get my

horse and while you're there, get Pine Leaf's also, she wanted to come with me when this new baby joins us," and turning back to Caleb she instructed him, "And you go to her lodge and let her know it's time."

The lodge of Broken Shield and Pine Leaf was a short distance away and Caleb hastened to do her bidding. Broken Shield and Caleb's mother were like brother and sister although they were just cousins, and his wife Pine Leaf was a former War Leader and Pipe Bearer with the Kicked in the Bellies clan of the Crow people. Broken Shield was the leader of the village or chief of this clan of the Northern Arapaho. Their son, Spotted Deer, was just over two summers old and was like his namesake always bouncing around and curious about everything. When Caleb neared their lodge, he saw Leaf working on a hide stretched on a frame as Spotted Deer pretended to help.

"Pine Leaf, Pine Leaf, Waters said to tell you it's time!"

Turning to face the source of the alarm, she asked, "Time? Time for what?"

"It's time, you know, my wife, she's having the baby!" replied Caleb with a frustrated expression coloring his face. "Come on if you're coming, Pa's already getting your horse." He turned away and started back toward the lodge of Laughing Waters. Pine Leaf stepped into her lodge, grabbed a nearby bundle, picked up her son and was on her way in pursuit of Caleb. As they neared the lodge of his mother, Caleb saw Waters swing up aboard her buckskin mare with nothing more than a handhold on the mare's mane. She always amazed her son with her many skills as a proven warrior and leader of her people. She was smiling at Pine Leaf when they approached, and watched as Leaf handed her son to Caleb and swung aboard her sorrel mare in the same way Waters had done.

Looking at Jeremiah, Waters instructed, "You two," pointing at Jeremiah and Caleb, "will be responsible for those two," pointing at Spotted Deer and her son, five-year-old Little John or as he was now known, Red Hawk. Jeremiah nodded his head in agreement and raised his hand to wave at the back of his wife as she kneed her horse to a canter toward the trail to the cabin. Caleb looked at his Pa and with evident exasperation said, "Well, come on, we ain't got all day!"

"Now hold your horses, son, I've got to go get my mount so you tend to the young'uns till I get back. It'll give you some good practice takin' care of kids," he chuckled.

The two youngsters were no strangers and had already occupied themselves with a small pile of river donies, or water smoothed stones, and were trying to make a pile to knock it down again. Little John had developed a protectiveness about Spotted Deer and the two always sat side by side no matter the activity. Caleb's nervousness and impatience kept him pacing back and forth between his appaloosa and the youngsters as he continued looking in the direction of the horse herd for his absent father. Although it was only moments, to Caleb it seemed like hours when Jeremiah returned and saddled up his long legged steel dust gelding. Soon, two men and two boys were on their way back to the cabin.

The usual way of childbirth for an Indian woman was a solitary event with the woman squatting next to a sapling to hold onto, and delivering the baby onto a blanket with no one in attendance. But Clancy had no inclination to follow the way of the Arapaho and was determined to have her baby at home, in bed, in the warm cabin. With hands gripping the small uprights of the log headboard, sweat dripping from her brow and a scrunched up face, Clancy panted heavily as Waters tended her needs. Already more than two hours in labor, Waters feared there was trouble with the delivery. Looking across the bed at Pine Leaf, the exchanged looks were observed by Clancy. Between the pains, she asked, "What? What's wrong? There's something wrong isn't there?" She caught her breath and suffered another excruciating pain.

"Try to breathe deep, take quick short breaths," instructed Waters.

"Ohh, Ohhh, unhhnnnn ah!" answered Clancy.

Pine Leaf pushed a portion of an old blanket under the legs of the struggling woman and looked again at Waters. A slight nod told her companion in labor that there was something she should see. Waters stood and bent over the prone form of Clancy and began an examination. Then looking at her daughter she said, "Yes, there is a difficulty. The baby is turned and it will be hard for him to come into this world. We must work to make it easier for him."

Waters instructed Clancy on changing her position and the two women helped her move higher on the pillows and re-position her legs. The pain struck again and she screamed, then took a deep breath and gripped the uprights tightly and following the instructions of Waters began to push rhythmically.

Caleb started to tether his mount to the top rail of the corral next to the tied-off horses of Waters and Leaf, but his Pa suggested, "We're gonna be a while so let's turn 'em out in the corral. You take care of yours then you can help with these two," as he nodded to the mounts of the women.

"But Pa, I gotta see how she's doin'!" pleaded Caleb, referring to his wife.

"They ain't gonna let you in there, that's women's work. We'll just have to wait until they come get us. Ain't nuthin' you can do anyway but just get underfoot. 'Sides, we got these young'uns to tend to."

Begrudgingly Caleb nodded his agreement and opened the gate to the corral to turn his mount in, unsaddled and removed the bridle and pushed him toward the lean to shelter. He returned to the tethered horses and led the two into the corral to repeat the process and watched as his Pa duplicated his efforts. The two boys were chasing each other with a handful of foxtail weeds and laughing all the while. As Caleb watched the boys playing, he remembered his youth in the woods of Michigan. The only son of the town doctor and his wife, Caleb took to the trees at every opportunity, whether he was climbing them and pretending to be an Indian scout, or running through them thinking he was a deer, the forest had always been his haven. At times it didn't seem that long ago, but other times it was two or three lifetimes ago. When his mom died in child-birth and his dad married Jeremiah's sister, he thought he would spend his lifetime following in his father's foot-steps. Then came the plague and his father died from tending the many folks stricken with typhus and his step-mom soon followed, his life took a major turn after his uncle Jeremiah kept a promise to his sister to take Caleb to live with him. After their long journey from Michigan to the tall timber of the mountains, Caleb thought he would live the dream of a life in the moun-tains with the Indians. It was a few years later that Jere-miah and Caleb found Clancy Mae, the only survivor of a Crow Indian attack on the small wagon train, and brought her home to be his new sister. Now as his wife of two short years, she lay in there giving birth to their first child.

Caleb shook his head in disbelief and Jeremiah noted his son's action and asked, "What's the matter son, whatcha thinkin' 'bout?"

"Oh, just rememberin' Pa. You know, all the way back to Michigan territory when you and Uncle Scratch came ridin' up to the cabin, the way you looked sittin' on your horse in your buckskins and me just a skinny kid in high water britches and barefoot. Seems like a hunert years ago, and now here we are in the mountains with the Indians and I'm about to become a dad myself. Unbe-lievable."

"Well, we've had some good years, and I know if my sister could see you now, she'd be mighty proud of the man you've become."

"Thanks Pa, that means a lot," then looking at the

boys running toward the creek said, "but we better catch them two or Ma's gonna have our hides!"

The two men caught the boys just as they were ankle deep in the backwater pool made by the turn of the creek. Catching them around the middle, the men packed them to the sandy bank and sat down. Jeremiah remonstrated the boys with, "Now you young 'uns don't go near the water without one of us a watchin' so if you wanna wade out there a little bit, fine, we'll be right here."

With his gaze traveling both upstream and downstream, his eyes came to rest on a wooden contraption set back from a sandbar a little way downstream. Turning to Caleb he said, "I see you been workin' the rocker a bit. Gettin' anything?"

"Yeah, I just do it ever now an' then, got some color. Got a couple o' bags back in the cabin. Hit a purty good streak the other day and brought out some nice nuggets. I think the big lode is just over yonder past that cut bank where that dry stream bed joins the creek. It was just after that rain we had and some water came down there and washed out that bit o' color. It wouldn't surprise me if we were to work our way back up that creek bed, we'd find a real nice pay streak."

Before Jeremiah could respond, they heard a call from the cabin. The men jumped up, grabbed the boys, and trotted back to the cabin each with a boy on his shoulders and laughing like a couple of braying mules. When Caleb saw the expression on Pine Leaf's face, he stopped and took her son, Spotted Deer, from his shoulders and the boy started running toward his mother. As she bent to pick up her son, she looked at Caleb with a deep sadness etched across her face and she slowly shook her head, and dropped her gaze.

"What's that mean? What's the matter?" he said as his long strides brought him to the front step where she stood.

"I'm sorry, Talks," she said using his Indian name, Talks to the Wind, "your son did not make it. The Great Spirit has him now."

"Nooo . . ." he groaned as he pushed the door open. Leaf grabbed his arm and said, "Be gentle, your woman lost a lot of blood. She is very weak."

Caleb pushed open the door to the bedroom and both women looked at him with sadness and fear in their eyes. He paused as he saw the still form in the tiny basinet he had fashioned with willows, and looked at the ash white face of his wife. Her red hair was tousled and her face had tear tracks among her freckles, her eyes were red with grief and her shoulders slumped in sadness. Two long strides brought him to her side and he knelt at the edge of the bed, leaned over and wrapped his arms around her shoulders and pulled her to him. Together they wept. Turning his head slightly to look at his Ma, Laughing Waters, he motioned for her to take the basinet and the baby from the room. Leaning back from the tight embrace, Caleb looked at Clancy and softly said, "I love you and I will always love you." And embraced her again and held her to his chest while she sobbed on his shoulder.

A BEAUTIFUL DAY IN THE MOUNTAINS USUALLY HAS A cloudless blue sky occasionally dotted with a few hawks or an eagle, a gentle breeze that carries the sweet smell of pine, the chuckle of a nearby stream cascading over the rocks in a hurry to the flatlands, and the sound of birds filtered through the trees. Today was a beautiful day. Jeremiah and Caleb sat side by side on what Jeremiah used to call his prayer log. Caleb looked through the break in the trees and let his gaze rove the distant valley below. Jeremiah absentmindedly scratched in the dirt before him with a snag of a stick.

"Pa, I just don't know what to do. She won't hardly talk to me and when she does she don't say much. She tries to hide her cryin' but I can hear her behind the bedroom door. And I feel so helpless. It's tearin' my heart out, Pa."

"Maybe what you need is a change of scenery," suggested Jeremiah.

"Whatchu mean? Go somewhere else? What good'd

that do? She's hurtin' inside, not outside."

"Yes, but everything she looks at reminds her of what happened and brings it all back. Sometimes it takes a different place, no reminders, to get your mind focused on the future and not the past."

"Are you sayin' we need to leave?" asked Caleb with a touch of confusion in his voice.

"Remember a couple years back, before you were hitched, and both of you were questioning your future and what you were gonna do? You went on that vision quest with your Grandfather and when you came back you knew what you were going to be doin' with your life."

"Oh yeah, I remember, and when I got back them outlaws had taken Clancy and I thought I'd never see her again."

"Yeah, but God brought her back to you and you've had a pretty good couple of years, haven't you?"

"Umhumm, until now," replied Caleb.

"Sometimes son, God has to turn our world upside down to shake us out of the corners we been hidin' in. When you were thinkin' 'bout your future back then, what else did you think you might like to try 'sides livin' here with us?"

"Well, both of us had thought about goin' back to Michigan territory or to the city, but that didn't really appeal to us. We also thought about maybe tryin' farmin' or ranchin' or sumpin' like that. I don't think I could really handle city livin'. Too many people for my taste."

"When my dad and I left Michigan territory and came out here, he had no idea what he would do, he just had to get away from where my mom died. He thought about becomin' a trapper or somethin' like that but I think he just wanted to see the mountains. It's a little different when you have a wife, but it's not like you'd have some prissy sissy of a woman taggin' along. She's mountain smart and country wise, and she's pretty savvy when it comes to people too. And you and I both know she's 'bout as good a shot as you are, and she's better with a bow. I imagine the two of you could handle just about anything that comes your way.

By the way, did you follow up that stream bed and see if there was any more nuggets up that-a-way?"

"Yeah, whenever she couldn't stand havin' me underfoot, I'd go to the rocker and do a little diggin' and I did walk up the stream bed a ways. It wasn't but maybe ten or so yards upstream there, I found an exposed vein that the high water would wash against and bring us some nuggets and dust down to the rocker. Come on, let me show you."

The two men walked over to the creek, waded across the shallows, and started up the dry stream bed. Arriving at the designated place, Caleb bent down and pushed aside a couple of larger stones he had placed there to obscure the exposed vein. A sizeable shoulder of white quartz was exposed and a spider web vein the size of two thumbs laced the opaque stone and glistened in the sunlight. Caleb looked over his shoulder to see the reaction of his Pa. Wide eyes greeted him and a whispered, "Holy Cow!" slipped from his Pa's lips.

Walking back to the cabin, both men were silent and thinking about the gold and the future. Jeremiah had no desire to leave the mountains and only used some gold to supplement the value of hides and furs when he traveled to the rendezvous for supplies. Never showing enough to pique the interest of others, but only using it when there was no other means of procuring the necessary supplies like powder, lead, salt and other trade goods. But he knew the gold could be both a curse and a blessing to his son if he were to leave the mountains and seek to establish a life elsewhere.

Caleb never allowed the gold to come into his thoughts whenever he considered leaving the mountains, his concern was more about where to go and what to do but now his thinking was focused on Clancy and what needed to be done for her. Almost a month had passed since the loss of the baby and Caleb had spent considerable time in prayer, but only for Clancy and not about any other possibility. *Well, God, I guess you and me gotta figger out the next step. It shore would be nice if you'd kinda step in here and give me a push in the right direction.*

As they approached the cabin they noticed two horses tethered to the rail beside the home and recognized the mounts as those of Scratch and his new bride, Walking Dove, Ezekiel's widow.

"Hey Pa, it's Scratch. Maybe he can cheer up Clancy, he always did have a way with her."

Scratch had fallen in with Jeremiah many years back when Jeremiah was on his vengeance quest to regain the gold stolen by the slave catchers that murdered Ezekiel. The two men became partners and traveled to Kentucky to fulfill his promise to Ezekiel to free his slavery bound family and back to Michigan territory where Caleb joined them. Affectionately referred to as Uncle Scratch, he had become part of the family and married Ezekiel's widow and moved into the village to become a part of the Arapaho clan.

Standing in the doorway, the scruffy mountain man nodded his head at the approaching men, and stepped down to greet his friends. "Wal, whatchu two up to? With them long faces yore sportin' you'd think you was on yore last leg." He leaned forward with an outstretched hand to shake with Jeremiah and his other arm corralled Caleb into a bear hug. Pushing the younger man away a bit, he looked him square in the eye and said, "Howya doin' squirt?"

"Oh, all right, Uncle Scratch, you know how it is."

"Yup, reckon I do, but yore man 'nuff to handle it. Yore woman needs ya now, so ya gotta man up and take care o' her."

"I'm tryin' Uncle Scratch, I'm tryin'"

"I know ya are boy, and you can do it, I'm certain sure."

Turning to Jeremiah, he winked his reassurance and tugged at his elbow to draw him aside with a nod toward Caleb that told him to give him room. Jeremiah said to his son, "You go on in, me 'n this ole coon'r goin' chew the fat a little."

Without a backward look, Jeremiah pushed open the door of the cabin and entered to find Waters, Walking Dove, and Clancy sitting at the table. All three women looked at the new arrival and motioned for him to join them. Pulling back the remaining chair, he slowly sat down and looked from one face to the other and began to feel like a cornered varmint. Waters began, "Son, we," sweeping her arm to include all three women, ". . . have been talking."

Caleb nodded his head, waiting for the verdict to come in from his jury of three women.

"And we agree, you and Clancy need to go from this place, find a new home. Maybe with new people and new things, and no memories, someplace where you can make new memories."

Caleb looked at Clancy as she dropped her gaze to the table in front of her and asked, "Is this what you want Clancy? To get away, go someplace new?"

Without looking at him, she nodded her head up and down, moved a hand to the table top to stroke the grain of the wood and dropped it back to her lap again. With a barely audible whisper she said, "I think so, could we?" and lifted her eyes to her husband, still red with weeping and tears held in the corners. Just seeing her this way brought tears to his own eyes and with a quick swipe with his shirt sleeve, he nodded his head and said, "Pa and I were just talkin' 'bout the same thing." Her eyes opened wide revealing a rim of white and said, "Really?"

"Yeah, we agreed it'd probably do us good. That don't mean we can't come back if we want to but maybe just some time away would help."

His response brought the first smile to her face that anyone had seen since before the loss. It was infectious and everyone at the table showed white teeth topped by tears on their cheeks. Waters rose from the table and said, "I will start something for our supper. You two need to take a walk and talk a little," she instructed. Caleb extended his hand as he rose and Clancy reached for his reassurance as they looked at each other smiling. Waters motioned for Dove to join her and the two women made busy at the counter, as Caleb and Clancy left the cabin.

Walking hand in hand the young couple made their way to Jeremiah's prayer log and sat down close to one another side by side. With his arm around Clancy's shoulder, Caleb asked, "Where do you think you'd like to go? Back to the city or just somewhere besides here?"

"I don't know, it's all kinda new to be thinkin' about. But I do like the idea of gettin' away. You don't mind do you?" she asked hopefully.

"Nah, even before we got hitched, we were talkin' about goin' somewhere's else, but I just don't rightly know where to go. I've thought about different things, we both have, but I ain't too particular. One place is as good as another, long's we're together," he answered with a smile and a squeeze of her shoulder.

"I heard you and Pa talk about Fort William and how that's where the wagon trains come through, maybe we could just go there and then decide. Who knows? Maybe we could join a wagon train like my family first did and go to Oregon or somewhere else. We don't have to decide that right now, we can just head that way and if we change our minds, well, we just point our horse's ears another direction and go. How's that sound?"

Caleb turned to see a smile on Clancy's face and a bit of mischievousness shining in her eyes and smiled as he responded, "Sounds fine to me. Let's go back to the house for supper and we'll share that with Pa and Ma and Scratch."

THE CABIN WAS FULL OF COMPASSION, companionship and comfort on this evening of anticipation. Chatter amongst the ladies drove the men and their full bellies to the porch and the star-filled night. Scratch filled his short stemmed clay pipe with his special blend of wild tobacco and cured leaves, grabbed the end of a thin stick with a glowing ember end and brought it to the small bowl, drew a deep breath and exhaled a cloud of thin blue-white smoke. The three men sat on well-placed logs that formed a triangle around the small fire pit that was often used for smoking meat. With flames reflecting from his eyes, Scratch asked, "So, Squirt, have you decided where and when yore a'goin'?"

Staring into the dancing flames, Caleb replied, "Not sure, Uncle Scratch. We talked a bit about goin' to Fort William and then decide. Maybe hook up with a wagon train headin' West or if she's of a mind, we could continue on East to the city, or someplace else, I guess. I'd thot 'bout headin' up to Fort Union and seein' 'bout doin' some trappin' but I don't think that's any kinda life with a woman by your side. Guess it's just gonna be catch as catch can."

"Well, son," started Jeremiah, ". . . the world's wide open to ya. You don't have ta decide until the time comes. I think every young man gets a hankerin' now and then to see what's waitin' on the other side o' the mountain. You were pretty young when you came West with us and you've experienced a lot more of life than many others your age, but there's still a lot to see."

It was a melancholy mood that captured the thoughts of the three men sitting around the fire. Thoughts of remembrance of past camp fires, trails traveled, lessons learned and life moments shared filled the eyes and minds of each one. Intermingled with memories were faces of friends and foes, trials faced and special moments together. Yet possibilities of youth crowded their minds with images of what could be or what might happen, adventures to experience and country to explore. The wanderlust that fills the heart of every man and drives many to conquer new heights often raises its head to chastise about unheeded opportunities. Neither Scratch nor Jeremiah would hinder their young charge from fulfilling his vision or calling but would do as they always did and provide any assistance and guidance that would enable the young man to realize every potential he possessed.

"Whatcha thinkin' 'bout doin' to get this hyar shindig underway?" asked Scratch, more as an offer to help than a nudge of curiosity.

"I figger whatever we do, money'd come in handy. I

thot I'd take some time to work out that seam of gold up the creek there to give us a bit of a poke to take with us. As thick as it is, and with what I already got, I don't think more'n a day or two would be needed. Then of course, all the usual stuff 'fore ya take out, you know, horses, tack, packs and such."

Looking at one another, Jeremiah and Scratch just nodded their heads in agreement, and the look in their eyes said they had done a good job of teaching this young man. Caleb had been a willing and eager student of the two experienced mountain men from the first day they met so many years ago in Michigan territory. With their trail side schooling regarding plants, animals, tracks and survival, Caleb realized that his wilderness education was a life-time of learning. He had surprised the men with his amazing ability to duplicate and mimic the sounds and calls of every animal and bird of the wild and this special ability had earned him his Arapaho name of He Who Talks to the Wind. That ability had repeatedly proven its worth during their many expeditions of hunting, whether for man or beast. The men continued their talk of the past and future well into the night until the fire burned low and bedrolls beckoned.

Walking Dove, Laughing Waters and Clancy worked silently together as they cleaned up after the evening meal. The glassy stares held by each woman did little to reveal the thoughts of reverie that swirled through the passages of their minds. Dove broke the silence with, "Sun of the Morning," she spoke pensively, "I have always thought that name fit you so well. Your hair that is just like the rising sun is so beautiful, but your name also speaks of each new morning as the beginning of a new day, and now, you and your husband will be going off together to start a new part of your life, just like the start of another new day." She spoke as she wiped off the rough board table and turned to look at the red headed girl seated at the end of the table. Clancy smiled at this wise woman of the people. Walking Dove had been a respected leader of the people since before she was married to Ezekiel, or Buffalo Thunder, the adopted father of Jeremiah. Caleb had considered her as a grandmother and often referred to her with that respected title and Clancy had grown in her love for this very special woman of her family. Dove's simple reference to a "new day" though simple in its reference was deep in meaning and purpose for Clancy, and the encouragement did not go unheeded by the girl.

Taking a seat with the other two women, Waters placed her hand on Clancy's and said in the direction of Dove, "I think this woman needs some more clothing for her trip, do you agree Dove?"

"Yes I do, and I think we could make her even more beautiful with a tunic and more," said Dove with a smile of collusion to which Waters answered with both a smile and a nod of her head. Clancy shared the joy and anticipation with the two women that had often been her mentors as well as friends and mother figures.

"And I think there are some other things we might do to help her," said Waters as she thought of the many remedies and applications for the plants and herbs of the field. Her teaching of Clancy had been somewhat sporadic but now took on a renewed urgency with the probability this might be her last opportunity to share her wealth of knowledge learned in her training as Shaman of the people. She sighed heavily as she thought of the limited time left with her adopted daughter. The women began to share special thoughts and plans for the remaining days and the many preparations yet necessary.

Mixed emotions inhabited the glen of busy workers undertaking their different tasks. Scratch had assumed the responsibility of tending to the horses and pack mule and was standing with the forefoot of Caleb's appaloosa between his thighs as he busily picked at the hoofs to prepare them for new horseshoes. Jeremiah sat on the edge of the porch step with a parfleche in his lap and saddle bags at his feet, as he worked on each article in turn. Caleb was busy at the gold in the creek bed and the women worked inside the house with their cutting, sewing, and beading of the different articles of buckskin clothing. The preparations were many, the thoughts more, and the days few, but busy work kept everyone actively involved and emotional conversation at an ebb.

As Caleb dug at the vein of gold embedded in the white and pink quartz, his eyes often watered and forced him to stop frequently and brush away the tears. This was not difficult work and his trips through the halls of memory oft sat him back on his haunches as he remembered his youthful trips into the woods, walks along the road with his Mom and Dad on the way to church, his travels with Jeremiah and Scratch, and his intimate moments with Clancy. The days ahead held promise that elicited excitement, but also concern that stirred the butterflies in his stomach, but the anticipation of adventure and partnership with his Clancy brought a broad smile to his face and he returned to the task at hand. With each strike of the mallet, the gold rich vein yielded large chunks of the soft ore and Caleb would break off most of the quartz that refused to lose its grip and drop the gold into his nearby parfleche. By mid-day his examination of the vein showed he had exhausted the readily available gold and to gain any more would require more work and time than he had available. Picking up the now heavy parcel, he stood and turned toward the cabin.

Seeing Jeremiah sitting on the stoop, Caleb joined his Pa and dropped the parfleche at his feet. Jeremiah pulled the gold heavy leather bag nearer, peered inside and looked at Caleb with wide eyes. "Boy, you've done well. This here's a mite of gold you got for yourself."

"Yeah, it's pretty heavy, but that don't mean I've got to take it all with me. I don't rightly know what I'd do with it anyway."

With a knowing chuckle and a sidelong glance at his adopted son, Jeremiah responded, "Well, when you're travelin' in this country and especially if you get into what they call civilization, you'll soon find out that money is a heap more important there than you'll ever find in the mountains." Standing and lifting the bag to his shoulder, Jeremiah motioned for Caleb to follow. Behind the tack shed, Jeremiah had constructed a make-do blacksmith forge complete with anvil and other tools used to work with metal for horseshoes and other needs.

"Get that fire goin' and I'll show you what I got in mind for this," instructed Jeremiah nodding toward the parfleche of gold.

The melancholy mood lifted as the women resumed their conversation of instruction to their willing student, Clancy. Waters had opened her leather pouch of mystery and displayed the many plants as she arranged them on the tabletop. Explaining where each one could be found, the primary and secondary application for each one, and how best to preserve them, she divulged a literal encyclopedia of knowledge for Clancy. Some were familiar, some totally new and some very mysterious, but the eyes and mind of the girl absorbed it all. Occasionally Walking Dove would look up from her work on the buckskins and add some bit of knowledge or tale of how she found and used the plants but the Shaman of the People, Laughing Waters, was the professor of this very special class in wilderness education.

THE MORNING SUNLIGHT PAINTED THE TOPS OF THE pines with a golden glow that announced a new day in the wilderness in the Wind River Mountains. The two appaloosas stood three legged at the hitch rail in front of the cabin while Caleb made repeated trips in and out carrying the packs, bedrolls, and saddle bags for the journey. The mule stared with disinterest as the young man and his two mentors packed the parfleches and leather panniers on the nonchalant mule.

Jeremiah spoke to Caleb with a cautionary tone, "Now, I've put false bottoms in your parfleches and saddle bags for the pouches of gold dust and nuggets, and those two smaller draw string pouches hangin' from your saddle horns and in front of your pommels have the "heavy" balls we made." He referred to their work at the forge when they melted the gold into the bullet molds, then dropped them into lead for a thin coating of lead. The balls would appear to be nothing more than spare molded musket balls but were actually solid gold.

"You're carryin' a pretty good store of gold with you and anyone that discovered that would be mighty tempted, so do your best to not let anyone know about it. And if you get to St. Louis, you can put it in the bank like I tol' ya, cuz I still got a pretty good account there and they'd be happy to help you out." Then reaching to a pouch hanging from his belt he held it out to Caleb and said, "Now this'll probly' take care of anything you need for a good spell and you won't even have to touch the gold," as he extended the pouch to Caleb. The young man pulled the drawstring and emptied the contents into his hand and was surprised to see the twenty double eagle gold coins, and he looked askance to his Pa. "That there's what we took off'n that outlaw that took Clancy a while back, you remember the last one we done in over by South Pass. He had that hangin' on his belt and I relieved him of the burden just 'fore we buried him. I figger it rightly belongs to you and Clancy anyway."

Scratch and Walking Dove had returned to the village the night before, leaving the good-byes to the family. Laughing Waters and Clancy stepped through the doorway and joined the men at the hitch rail. Clancy walked to Caleb's side and extended her arms to him holding a recently finished buckskin jacket. As she held it up, he could see the beautiful bead work across the chest yoke, the fringe that fell from the yoke and shoulders and cascaded down the length of the arms. Small patterns of blue and white beads and white porcu-pine quills decorated the pocket flaps, but the most noticeable was the grizzly bear claws that were inter-spersed with the fringe that marked the yoke from the shoulders. The pattern of beads and quills on the yoke matched that of the pocket flaps and accented the bear claws. As she shook the jacket, he realized she wanted him to put it on. He turned around and she helped slip it on her man's broad shoulders and smoothed it out across his back. As he turned around, he saw she wore an exact duplicate that matched his in every detail. As he fingered the claws on her jacket's yoke, she said, "Well, I helped you kill it so I deserve some of the claws too!" The two turned and faced Jeremiah and Laughing Waters as the proud parents smiled at their two adopted children. Laughing Waters held her hands to her mouth and her eyes filled with tears. Jeremiah smiled broadly and casually wiped the water from his cheeks as the tears escaped his eyes.

Clancy stretched out her arms and reached for Waters and the two women hugged and held each other for a long moment with whispered words shared. Caleb and his Pa hugged each other like a pair of grizzlies as they slapped each other on the back. Clancy broke her embrace and pushed Caleb aside so she could hug her Pa as Caleb turned to Waters and lifted his Ma off the ground as he hugged her tight. He turned and took the reins of his and Clancy's mounts from the rail, held her horse while she mounted and he followed suit. Jeremiah held the lead rope for the mule up to Caleb and said, "Now don't either one of you get so far away that you forget your way back, now ya' hear?"

"Sure Pa, we won't forget. And you'll be hearin' from us, ya never know, you might look up one day and there we'll be," reassured Caleb, more for himself than his folks.

"You take care of that girl!" instructed Waters to her son with a firm look.

"You know I will, course she'll probably spend as much time takin' care of me," admitted Caleb.

The two adventurers kneed their horses and turned to the downhill trail and as Clancy had said, pointed the ears of their horses to the trail that would lead them to their tomorrows. Silence marked the way for both as they lifted a hand and turned in their saddles to get a last glimpse of their folks standing on the front step of the cabin as they waved goodbye. As the trees obscured their view they turned in their saddles and examined their hearts and the decision to leave the only home they had known for the last several years. What lay before them, neither knew, but the anticipation of new adventures and vistas drew them on, such was the excitement that prevailed in their thoughts and the constant tug of heart strings threatened to change their minds.

The flutter of wings as a covey of sage hens took flight captured their attention and Caleb echoed their bubbling gobble as they fled. Clancy giggled at the sounds from her man and shook her head at his habit of talking to the animals.

Descending the switch-back trail brought them to the creek side path by the Popo Agie. The deep cut of the canyon walls framed the distant valley below them and the blue sky that topped the narrow vista promised a good day for their travel. Caleb led the way and chose to bypass the shallow red walled canyon and trail that would take them to South Pass. The memories of Clancy's kidnapping and subsequent rescue were not welcome thoughts and Caleb chose instead to follow a route that would take them beyond the red clay canyon and its reminders of a time best forgotten. Clearing the rim rock and foothills, he bore South East with the goal of the Sweetwater creek as a site for the first night's camp. The horses were fresh and the trail easy so Caleb chose to continue their trek without a mid-day break. Now in the flats and rolling hills pocked with sage brush, prickly pear and Cholla cactus, buffalo grass and plenty of rabbits, coyotes and antelope, the couple rode side by side and shared each discovery of animals and plants with simple comments or a nod of the head. Simple times and precious moments together to be treasured for what they were, special and rare.

Late afternoon saw them wading the shallow Beaver creek and as the sun was cradled in the distant mountains, they spotted a likely campsite on the near bank of the Sweetwater. A cluster of cottonwood, a grassy knoll, and creek side willows offered a welcome for the now tired couple and their animals. As Caleb dropped from his mount, he stretched his weary legs to regain his strength and balance, and reached up to help Clancy dismount. She walked to the pack mule and lifted the pack with the cooking utensils and some foodstuffs while Caleb removed the saddles, bridles and packs from the animals. Clancy busied herself with the evening meal while Caleb picketed the animals and stretched out their bedrolls. The tasks were familiar and occupied their thoughts until Caleb seated himself on a log by the fire and watched his wife as she prepared the stew in the pot. As he watched he voiced his thoughts, "You know, I sure am glad you're my wife. Every time I look at you I have to thank the good Lord that we're together."

Clancy stopped stirring and looked at her husband with a smile as she responded, "I can't imagine my life without you husband and I sure am glad we're together too!" Then returning to her task at hand, she smiled at the thought of her life with Caleb and the adventure they were embarked upon.

THE DAWN PAINTED THE LOW HANGING CLOUDS WITH shades of red and pink with a touch of orange that tickled the topsides. Glancing at his wife, Caleb smiled at the reflected colors that blended with her Irish red hair and her smiling green eyes. She enjoyed the colors of the sunrise and basked in the warmth of the slow rising orb that spread the wealth of colors across the nearby shallow ripples of the Sweetwater. It promised to be a great day to enjoy the wonders of the Creator. Following the East flowing river, their chosen trail wound its way along the grassy bottom of the wide spreading valley. Near the waterway, grass was abundant and green, but just a short distance away, the plains were varying shades of brown and muted blue green of the sage. The terrain was deceiving with an appearance of flatness, but the rolling hills and cap-rock rimmed flat topped plateaus and mesas broke the monotony of the vista. Herds of antelope stared at the passing wanderers and big footed long eared jackrabbits scurried away attracting the attention of golden eagles and coyotes searching for their next meal. It was a pleasant spring day with little dust in the air or on the trail beneath them, fresh air that whispered past as it sought escape from the snowcapped mountains behind them.

Out of habit they traveled the trail that nestled near the stream and below the nearby ridges. Without thought they avoided the ridges and hill crests knowing it was safer to travel new country in obscurity. This was territory that was hunted by the Utes, Cheyenne, and even the Crow. Although the Arapaho were allies with the Cheyenne and some of the Crow clans, the Ute were known enemies. And now without the protection of a nearby Arapaho clan, Caleb knew he and Clancy were alone in the land of many different peoples, not all of whom were friendly. The sound of a gunshot startled the travelers and both reined up immediately. Caleb motioned to Clancy with an open palm the direction he thought the sound came from and he received an affirmative head nod in agreement. Slipping his rifle from its scabbard Caleb dropped to the ground and handed the reins of his mount to Clancy. As silent as a stalking coyote, he made his way to the crest of the nearby hillock. Hiding behind a small clump of sage, he surveyed the plains before him. Two horses stood ground tied, while two men in buckskins busied themselves at the carcass of a downed antelope. Sound carries in the wide open and Caleb strained to listen to the talk.

"Wal, this ain't much, but them pilgrims back yonder'll still be glad to sink thar teeth into some fresh meat," came the words from under a scraggly bush of a beard.

"Yah, ver gonna hafta carry it b'hind our saddles, ain't no tree ta hang it from," responded the larger of the two men. This one had thick blond hair protruding from a floppy felt hat and a thick yellow beard that covered most of his chest. Both men were in well-worn and soiled buckskins and worked with experienced hands at the butchering. Within moments the goat of the plains was gutted, skinned, deboned and the meat wrapped in the tan and white hide for packing behind the saddle. As the men stood, the blond towered over his much smaller companion, but their attire and manner told of experienced mountain men. Caleb slowly stood to reveal himself with his Hawken cradled at the ready.

"Whoa . . . whar'd you come from younker?" asked the scraggly one.

"Back yonder a piece. What are you two doin' out here in the middle of nowhere?" quizzed Caleb.

"Yah, ve be gettin' some meat for dem pilgrims back at the train. Ve're guidin' dem to the shinin' mountains and beyond. But you are here too, in da middle ov novhere," the statement was as much of a question as not and the men waited for a response. The larger man held the pack of meat lightly in his left hand and his right cradled a well-used Hawken. Caleb glanced at the smaller man and noted his rifle was in his left hand and held lightly at his side.

"We're headin' for Ft. William," responded Caleb without telling more than necessary.

"Ve? I don' see nobody else."

"That's right, and you won't till we're satisfied. This train you're talkin' about, are they very far back?"

"Nah," said the shorter of the two, "We're scoutin' fer 'em and we just left 'em this mornin'. They're mighty short of fresh meat and we're fetchin' 'em some. Say, if'n yore headin' thataway, how 'bout you takin' this hyar meat to 'em and we'll be able to keep on goin' on our scoutin'?"

"I spose' we could do that. How many of 'em are there?"

"Ah, we only got nineteen wagons, lost a couple the other side of the fort to some Sioux."

The big man approached Caleb with the parcel of meat and as he neared he dropped the hide and turned to fetch his mount. Over his shoulder he said, "Now, you be sure'n get that to dem, dere be some younguns' that'r mighty hungry." As they mounted, they started out and asked, "Ya see any injun sign?"

"Nothin' fresh, but this is prime country for Cheyenne, Ute and even some Crow. If you run into any Arapaho, just tell 'em you met Talks to the Wind and you'll be all right."

Both men turned to look at the young man with curiosity and asked, "That be you?"

Caleb just nodded his head and bent to pick up the parcel of meat. A casual wave sent the men on their way as Caleb returned to the waiting Clancy. As he explained to the redhead about the meat and the wagon train, her eyes lit up with the expected meeting of new people and a broad smile painted her face. "Did he say there were some young'uns that were hungry? Maybe we oughta try to get some more meat for them don't you think?"

Caleb's answering smile and nod of the head expressed both his agreement and understanding of his sympathetic wife. He mounted up and they continued on the riverside trail. With occasional rolling hills and rocky outcroppings, the river wound its way through the shallow valley taking the path of least resistance. The winding stream that occasionally overran its banks with mountain snow melt or heavy spring rains, provided ample water for the grassy flats. The water and graze were magnets for herds of antelope, deer and buffalo and the two travelers kept a wary eye for any game that would supplement the meager supply they now carried.

A nearby round top hill shielded the travelers from a wide bend of the river, but the sharp ears of Clancy warned Caleb to pull up. The familiar grunts of a buffalo caught their attention prompting the duo to ground hitch their mounts, take their rifles and move to the crest of the hill to see what was on the other side. Lying on their bellies they were able to see without being seen and they observed a small herd of buffalo enjoying the graze and morning sun's warmth. Two young bulls were sparring with each other and kicking up a bit of a dust cloud. Looking to one another, they agreed to take the young bulls in preference to the cows that suckled their young. Two well placed shots dropped the pair and scattered the rest of the small herd enabling the shooters to gather their mounts and start the butchering. Their experienced hands made short work of the arduous task and while Clancy finished deboning the last bull, Caleb cut the tallest of two sapling cottonwood to fashion a travois. Using the one hide to make the support for the travois, the meat was piled high and covered with the second hide. With their work complete and a quick wash up in the shallows of the Sweetwater River, they mounted up to find the wagon train.

No more than a quarter of an hour passed before the sighting of the white bonnet on the lead wagon of the train. Two men were horseback in the lead and the wagons stretched out behind like the white bones of a sun bleached skeleton. When the leaders spotted Caleb and Clancy, they gigged their horses to a trot to meet up with the unexpected travelers. After the preliminary greetings and Caleb's explanation of meeting their scouts, the leaders introduced themselves as Dan Russell and Doug Barham, the wagon master and his right hand man.

"So you met up with Dag and Gabby. I'm surprised that Gabby didn't talk your arm off, he's usually pretty hard to get shut up," said Dan.

Caleb just smiled and explained, "Well, it's usually a little uncomfortable talkin' with strangers, especially out here where everybody is suspect, but the big guy did most of the talkin'."

"One thing for sure, our folks are gonna greatly appreciate that meat. Mighty kind of you to share with us, I think we'll go 'head on and stop for our noonin'. Won't you join us for a meal?"

Looking at Clancy and seeing the smile of expectancy spreading, Caleb answered the wagon master, "I spose we can do that. It's been a while since we met up with anyone and I think my wife is kinda hungry for conversation."

When the wagons drew up into a large semi-circle,

the families were instructed to join the two hunters to get a share of meat for their supply. Happy faces and cheerful greetings wrapped the two in a welcome and appreciation bundle that both enjoyed. Clancy was especially blessed with the smiles and hugs from the youngsters, of which there were many. Accepting an invitation from a family to join them for a meal, Caleb and Clancy were pleased and enjoyed the shared bounty. When the children, four of them, found out that Clancy had lived with the Indians, she was overwhelmed with questions but enjoyed sharing her life's experiences. To know that Clancy had also come West on a wagon train filled the children with rapt wonder.

"And where are you going now?" asked the oldest girl, Ruby.

"Well, we really haven't decided, but we might go to St. Louis, because we've never been to a big city. But we might also find a home somewhere in the mountains, it really is all up to God."

The mother of the brood cast a quick glance at Clancy at the mention of God and her mouth opened slightly as if she were about to ask a question, then stopped and turned away. But as if a second thought came and courage rose, the woman turned to Clancy and asked, "How can you say it's up to God, when you have lived with the heathen Indians that attack and murder every white man they see?" The vehemence and hatred spilled out of the woman like an overflow of a sour well.

Taken aback by the attack, Clancy slowly responded, "Yes, there are some Indians that do that, just like there are whites that do that. It was a Crow raiding party that attacked our wagons and killed my parents, but it was an Arapaho party that rescued me. And it was because of those things that I came to know Christ as my personal Savior when Jeremiah, a white man that lived with the Arapaho and known as White Wolf, and his son who is now my husband, told me about the grace and forgiveness of our Lord Jesus. Yes, I could have been bitter, but if that hadn't happened, I might have never come to know Christ. You see, there are good and bad men and women in any group of people and we shouldn't condemn them all because of the action of a few."

The mother, Mildred, looked at Clancy with wonder and then argued, "But you don't understand, the Sioux attacked our wagon train and my son, my twelve-year-old son Daniel, was killed. He was too young to die!"

"And both my parents and everyone else in our small wagon train was killed and only I lived but I knew I couldn't dwell in the past and now I have all my life to look forward to and if I were to die, I know I'm going to heaven. Do you know that, Mildred?"

That simple question was the beginning of a much longer conversation that resulted in Mildred being comforted by a woman much younger in years but older in wisdom and compassion. By sharing with the mother of four and the children, Clancy was able to tell how Christ died to pay the price for their sin to give them the opportunity to receive the free gift of salvation. And the redheaded Irish girl led the mother and her four daughters in the simple prayer to ask for God's forgiveness and to receive the free gift of eternal life. After the group prayer, the girls asked Clancy if they would go to Heaven to which she answered, "If you meant the prayer when you asked Christ to forgive you and save you, then yes, the Bible says in Romans 10:13 that when you die you will go to heaven."

Almost on que, the wagon master yelled "Wagon's Ho" and the family had to jump to and finish loading the wagon so they wouldn't get left behind. With hugs all around, the now smiling family waved good-bye to Clancy and Caleb and Mildred shouted over her shoulder, "I'll never forget you! Thank you, thank you so much!" Clancy answered with a smile and a wave and a tear in her eye.

THE STAR STUDDED CANOPY HELD CLANCY'S attention as she lay with hands behind her head and eyes wide to search for their star at the tip of Orion's sword. Finding the three bright lights of the hunter's belt, she lifted her hand and traced the sword to its tip to find their star. When they were young and full of dreams, the two lovers had looked at the night sky and Caleb had told her how to find that star and it was then he proclaimed it was "their star." She smiled in the darkness at the memory of youth that seemed so long ago. *So much has happened since then. It seems like a lifetime ago, and now we're on the run from other memories.* A tear made its way down her cheek and she wiped it away feeling the coolness of the night breeze. Turning to her side with her back to Caleb, she prayed, *God, show us where to go, what to do. It hurts so much and I know Caleb feels the loss just like I do and I don't want him disappointed in me. Will we ever have children of our own, maybe a little girl like those on the wagon train or a boy to follow after his daddy.* Sleep finally captured the sad heart of the redhead and she relaxed in her slumber.

The crackle of the rekindled fire chased the sleep from her eyes and she sat up and stretched her arms overhead and yawned. Smiling at Caleb as he busied himself with the fire and the coffeepot, she said, "Well, you're mighty busy this morning. What got into you?"

He smiled back at his sleepy headed wife with the tussled red hair going in every direction and replied, "I thought we'd get an early start and maybe we can make the fort in a couple days."

"Really? That soon? I thought we were farther away than that."

"I'm thinkin' if we cut across to the North Platte and catch the Medicine Bow River South East, that'll get us over near the Laramie and we can follow it straight into the fort. See some new country thataway too. I been down through here with Pa and Scratch when we was huntin' buffalo and he told me all about it. We'll go North of the Medicine Bow mountains and swing South of the Laramie mountains and just follow the river to the fort. Two days, maybe three at most."

The chosen trail was non-existent and Caleb relied upon his own reckoning. It had been several years since he and his Pa together with Uncle Scratch had hunted this country. Unlike the flat plains with small rolling hills, this terrain was marked by high rising hog backs with sharp up thrusts of granite, hillsides littered with massive boulders and a scattering of juniper, pinion and oak brush. The prickly pear and Cholla cactus made their home where nothing else would grow and the pink and yellow buds promised a splash of color when the blossoms made their debut. Hidden in some rock piles would be an occasional cluster of hedgehog cactus that would provide a touch of purple to the landscape. The going was a little slower but the change in the terrain provided a break in the monotonous travel of the flats.

Keeping the high ridges off his right shoulder, Caleb soon had them at the banks of the North Platte and crossing the shallow but clear running stream promised a shady noon respite in a cluster of aged cottonwood amidst a grassy park like setting. The typical nooning for the couple consisted of jerky or pemmican and coffee with the sharing of thoughts and possibilities.

"So, after visiting with all those folks on the wagon train, have you been thinking a bit more on where you'd like to go?" inquired Caleb.

"Actually I'm thinking more about the city. Listening to the women talk about their lives, visiting the cities seemed to be a common dream of most of them. Maybe it was because of the hard lives they've had working on the farms and such, but whenever they talked about the city their faces lit up with the possibilities the big city offered."

"Well, the only big city I know about is St. Louis. I've never been there, but I've heard folks talk about it. And there's Sante Fe, but that's not the same, it's more of a trading town or something but not a big city. But we've got a ways to go before we decide. Maybe we'll meet up with somebody at the fort that can tell us more," surmised Caleb. Although he wasn't prone to go to the city, he was willing to do whatever was necessary to fulfill the wishes of his beloved wife. The memory of her grieving over the loss of the baby still brought tears to his eyes both for her and the loss of the child. All he wanted was for her to be happy and he was willing to do whatever necessary to make that a reality.

The afternoon's journey continued to the South East and followed the meandering Medicine Bow River. Caleb pointed to the South and told Clancy of the distant Medicine Bow Mountains. "I remember when we came down here a couple years back, we were following a big herd of buffalo. Over yonder to the West of those mountains there's a real pretty valley that's full of lush grass and lots of animals. We spotted a sizeable herd of wild horses, a bunch of elk and that herd of buffalo headed thataway too. Maybe someday we'll come back and I can show you that valley, it'd be a good place to make a home, I think."

As dusk was settling over the rugged ridges and placid valleys, the Medicine Bow river took a bend to the South and the grassy plain on the far side of the bend beckoned the couple to make camp for the night. While Caleb hobbled their mounts and made camp, Clancy surprised him with a supper of Dutch oven biscuits, boiled Buffalo tongue, and baked Yampa root. A very full and satisfied Caleb stretched out with his feet to the campfire and leaned back against a large boulder, patted his stomach, and smiled at his bride as she walked to his side. Seating herself next to him, she said, "So, did you like that supper?"

"Yes ma'm. That was quite a feast, those poor folks in the big city ain't never had nothin' like that, I'll bet."

"Maybe not, but to listen to those women talk, they sure liked going to those high falutin' eatin' places and havin' somebody wait on 'em hand and foot."

"Ah, them city slickers just like somebody caterin' to 'em cuz they're too lazy to fix it their own selves, I reckon."

With a jab in the ribs to her husband, Clancy started to rise but Caleb pulled her back to his side and started smothering her with kisses. She giggled and acted like she wanted to get away but it was obvious she was enjoying the attention. It wasn't that often that Caleb treated her like a woman instead of a traveling partner and she liked the reminder of being loved and cherished.

"If you'd let me go, we can get this mess cleaned up and maybe get a little sleep tonight," she suggested.

"Oh, all right. If you're gonna be like that. I suppose you want me to help you with all that too, don'tcha?"

"Or you could do it all and I could turn in and stare at the stars like you do."

The two lovers quickly finished the camp chores, checked on the horses and mule, banked the fire and crawled in the bedroll. Wrapped in each other's arms, they looked at the beautiful star filled sky and whispered sweet nothings to one another and soon drifted off to sleep with individual thoughts about their future. The night sounds of a distant coyote calling for his mate, a nearby bull frog bragging about his singing, a great Horned Owl asking questions of the darkness, and the constant chatter of crickets gave the travelers reassurance of their solitude and safety and gave comfort to their slumber.

The two or three days that Caleb had estimated turned into three and a half days of travel before they neared the fort. Following the Laramie river, their trail turned to the North East as they enjoyed the views of the Laramie Mountains to the North and the flats of the prairie to the South. It was just after nooning on the fourth day that they sighted the distant high-rising adobe walls of the fort. As they neared the fort they saw several hide lodges to the East of the walls and the herds of horses of the Indians and fort alike were lazily grazing in the grassy meadow to the North of the palisade. The travelers crossed the Platte just upstream of the confluence with the Laramie and headed to the gates of the fort. With a heavy sigh, Caleb looked at the fort and back at his wife, noticing a broad smile of expectancy spreading across her face. He was certain she had set her sights on going to St. Louis and he had resigned himself to fulfilling her wishes.

Well, the decision's been made, now all I gotta do if figger out how we're gonna get it done, wistfully thought Caleb.

APPROACHING THE FORT FROM THE UPSTREAM SIDE the couple was surprised to see a gathering of freight wagons loaded with hides. Several teamsters were leading mule teams to the pasture while others tended to the wagons and their loads. The wagons were lined out side by side and the hides were piled high above the racks. Although early in the season, they were probably the first of what would be many mule teams packing out the much in demand buffalo hides. The industrial centers of the East had discovered the heavy leather made from the buffalo was ideal for the drive belts of the heavy machines used in the factories. The massive herds of buffalo in the plains and the West were proving to be a bonanza for the hide and fur traders as the market for beaver pelts had declined with the rise in popularity of silk for the top hats of the day. Fur companies like Rocky Mountain Fur and American Fur Company had turned their focus on pelts of mink, otter, muskrat, coyote, wolf and cougar with a premium paid for the readily available buffalo.

The main gates stood wide open and the entire fort reminded Caleb of a beehive with traders, trappers and Indians walking to and fro carrying bundles of hides or trade goods. Outside the Sutler's a small cluster of loud and boisterous buck skinners lifted clay jugs of trade whiskey as they tried unsuccessfully to harmonize on a mountaineer's ballad. The side wall of the trading center supported a passed out grey bearded man sitting next to a small puddle of his own vomit. As an Indian warrior and his woman exited the Sutler's, they looked up at Caleb and Clancy as the couple were tying their mounts and mule to the hitch-rail and nodded their heads as they admired the beaded buckskin jackets worn by the pair. Caleb nodded his head in acknowledgment and reached for the arm of his wife as they stepped into the Sutler's to replenish their supplies.

"Howdy there, folks! Looks like you two just came down from the mountains. What can I do ya fer?" asked a red cheeked and red nosed, bald headed apron wearing cheerful man from behind his counter.

"Hello," extending his hand in greeting, "I'm Caleb Thompsett and this is my wife Clancy. We're needin' a few supplies and maybe a little information," stated Caleb. "We're headin' East and thought we'd find out about any uprisings or whatever that we might need to keep a watch out for, have you heard anything of the sort?"

"Well, not so much. There was a bunch went through here a few days back and they lost a couple o' wagons to a

Sioux raidin' party, but that ain't unusual. Ain't heard nuthin' 'bout any o' them Pawnees or anythin' else, but it's early in the season. Some o' them young bucks are still hangin' out in their villages and ain't got no raidin' parties goin' yet, but I'm sure we'll hear 'bout some with the warm weather comin' on us like it is. Now, what else can I do ya fer?"

"Lemme see, we're needin' some salt, sugar, coffee, galena, one o' them small kegs of powder, couple tins of caps, better make it three tins, . . . "

As Caleb continued with his list of needed supplies, Clancy walked down the counter and eyed a stack of bolts of cloth, absent mindedly ran her hand across the colorful bolts, lifted her eyes to the rows of canned goods and other supplies and let her imagination picture the stores of the big city and what wonders awaited. She walked outside and stood near the hitch rail and surveyed the interior of the fort with her eyes taking in the block-house that towered over the front gate and the others on opposite corners, the residence of the bourgeois against the back wall and the other structures against the walls that housed the supplies and accommodated other workers.

The activity of the workers and visitors seemed to hold to a leisurely pace as this was more of a stopover for repairs and rest for most travelers. Clancy turned to see Caleb exit the Sutler's with an arm full of packages bound for the packs on the mule. She readied the packs and unburdened her husband as she packed away the supplies in the leather panniers and parfleches. Caleb's second trip was equally burdensome but the pair made short work of packing the supplies away. Underneath the last parcel, Clancy discovered a leather sheath holding a new razor sharp Bowie knife. Looking askance at a now smiling Caleb, she realized it was for her to replace her well used Green River butcher knife. She had often admired and borrowed Caleb's Bowie and thought she would like to have one, but this unexpected gift was a pleasant surprise. She gave Caleb a big hug of thanks and she knew exactly how she would carry this gift, with two shoulder straps, it would rest between her shoulder blades beneath her tunic with the handle within easy reach.

As Caleb reached for the appaloosa's tethered reins, a tall barrel chested man clad in buckskin breeches, a Lindsey Woolsey plaid shirt with a buckskin vest straining at the antler tipped buttons and a knit cap stretched across coal black hair that tumbled over his collar and a thick black beard that sought to cover his open collared shirt, a broad smile that let loose a deep voice that seemed to echo from the far wall of the stockade said, "Hey thar young'un, the Sutler said you two was maybe lookin' to hook up with a wagon train or sumpin' that was headin' East. That right?" The greeting of 'young'un' didn't surprise or offend Caleb as he kept a clean shaven face that revealed his years.

"Uh, maybe so, we are headed East, that's a fact," answered an uncertain Caleb.

"Lookin' at yore outfit, 'pears you come from the mountains. Are you any good at makin' meat?"

"We've done a bit of huntin'" replied Caleb, still not sure where this confab was leading.

"Wal, iffn' you think you could do 'nuff huntin' to feed my crew, you'd be welcome to join us. We lost our guide and hunter a way back to some cussed Utes that jumped us. We're headed back to St. Louie with this hyar mule train and I'm certain shure it'd be safer travelin' with a big bunch iffn any them Pawnee or Sioux decide they wanted a scalp or two. Whatcha think, can ya handle it?"

Caleb looked to Clancy and a slight nod gave her answer. Turning back to the big man he said, "Sounds like you got yourself a couple hunters."

"My names McIntosh, most folks just call me Mac. I'm leadin' this bunch of pilgrim teamsters. They ain't good fer much but handlin' them mules and a few of 'em can shoot a mite. But if you stay out ahead of us, you can keep us in meat and give us a word if we have to have a set-to with any them Injuns. We'll pay you each a dollar a day and if'n you get a buffler or so on the way, you'll get paid extry fer the hides. We'll be leavin' first thing in the mornin' but if'n you wanna head out sooner, we'll foller along."

A handshake sealed the deal and the couple mounted up and turned to leave the fort. Over his shoulder Caleb told Mac, "We'll stay on the North side of the Platte and leave any meat hangin' in plain sight." A wave from the ham hock fists of the big man acknowledged the comment as he turned to tend to his last minute re-supply. The couple exited the fort and pointed their mounts to pass nearby the teepees of the Indians. They were Cheyenne and as the duo passed by the warrior they saw earlier approached with uplifted hand to speak with them.

"I see by your coat and moccasins; you have been with the Arapaho. Do you know them?"

"Yes. I am Talks with the Wind, this is Sun of the Morning," said Caleb as he motioned to Clancy. "We are part of the band of Broken Shield who is the son of Black Kettle, who was my grandfather."

A broad smile crossed his face as he nodded his head, "I remember you. You came through our village with your grandfather when you were on a vision quest to the Medicine Wheel. My son is also named Black Kettle; do you remember?"

Caleb dismounted and clasped forearms with the man and smiled as he said, "Yes, I remember. You made us welcome in your village."

White Buffalo looked at Caleb's jacket and touched the bear claws in admiration then turned to look at Caleb. "These are of our totem, the Grizzly. You took this one?"

A guilty smile prefaced his response, "Well, I shot him, but my wife gave the kill shot and dropped him at my feet. So, we shared the claws to remember." It was then that White Buffalo noticed the matching jacket of Clancy's and the claws that hung from her yoke in the same pattern as that of Caleb. He nodded his head in admiration and said, "Not many men have a woman that can kill a Grizzly. You must be careful with her, if she can kill a Grizzly, what would she do with you?" he stated with a broad smile.

Mounting his horse, Caleb said his good-byes as White Buffalo, now joined by his wife, waved to the departing duo. Clancy gigged her horse to take the lead and sat erect with pride to emphasize her enjoyment of the praise she received regarding the slaying of the Grizzly. *I ain't ever gonna live that down! It'd probably been better if ole Ephraim had eaten me, at least I wouldn't be embarrassed to tell it.* As dusk settled on the nearby hills, the duo broke out of the narrow canyon of the Platte as it opened to the rock rimmed bluffs and towering mesas that framed the vista of the broad expanse of plains before them. It was a good place to make their camp near the bank of the Platte, well protected from the wind, shaded by the cottonwood and with ample graze for the animals.

Twelve heavy wagons were each pulled by four to six mules and handled by an experienced teamster. Eight workers for helping with the loads and the wagon master meant twenty-one hungry men to provide meat for every day. As Caleb and Clancy soon found out, these men could eat a lot of meat. The numbers soon tallied to about two deer or three antelope per day or one buffalo every three or four days. The trail that many were now calling the Oregon or Emigrant trail was plentiful in game but only if it could be found. The pair of hunters knew they would be more successful at early morning or evening near the river, but they would often ride well away from the trail to find the herds of antelope or buffalo. By keeping the pack mule with them, they had little need of staying too near the mule train, but they were careful not to get too far away in the event of a sighting of a raiding party of Sioux or Pawnee.

By the third day out, a routine had been established. The couple would ride about an hour or two ahead of the train, take any available game, dress it out and hang it from any nearby trees within sight of the train and continue their scouting and hunting. Occasionally the train would catch up to them before they finished hanging the meat and the couple would often join the crew for the nooning or the evening meal. Always camping away from the train, the duo preferred their privacy and as Clancy said, "The fresh air beats the smell of all those hides and the teamsters don't smell too sweet either."

Several days passed with the monotony of the daily hunt, endless plains of flat or rolling hills, wide but shallow Platte River waters, and nothing of interest. Ten days into their journey, Clancy stood in her stirrups to improve her view and pointed East as she said to Caleb, "Is that a wagon train comin'?" In the distance on the opposite side of the river, the white skeletal backbone of a wagon train wound its way Westward. From the slight rise the two shaded their eyes as they watched in wonder the snake like movement of the large wagon train. Too many to count from their promontory, they gigged their horses toward the flat and the banks of the Platte to view the pilgrims that sought to populate the West. Caleb sat with hands on top of one another resting on the saddle horn and slowly shook his head. "There's so many of 'em, I wonder where they're all agoin'?"

"Well, don't they call this the Oregon Trail? They must be goin' to Oregon," answered Clancy.

"I hope they keep goin' cuz there's already too many people in this part o' the country. Why, just think of all the people we've run into on this trip already! You'd think there ain't nobody left back East!" proclaimed the young man dejectedly.

Clancy looked at her husband, smiled and shook her head at his absurdity and responded, "Caleb, you know that ain't so. Why the way I heard it, there's more people in St. Louis than we've seen in our whole lives. Can you imagine that?"

The wagon train continued on the trail as an outrider rode to the opposite bank and waved at the visitors. The answering wave from Caleb prompted the rider to cross the shallow river and join the duo as they sat observing the passage. When he pulled up in front of the pair, he tipped his hat and said, "Howdy folks, I'm Rafe Dougherty, I'm scoutin' for that there train you see yonder. Where 'bouts you folks comin' from?"

"We're coming from back yonder," said Caleb motioning toward their back trail, ". . . and we're headin' thataway."

With a chuckle and a shake of his head he responded, "Guess that was a mite nosy, wasn't it? Well, what I'm askin' about is if you had any run-ins with Injuns or anything?"

"We're ten days out of Ft. John," the newer name for what had been Ft. William," and we've seen nothing of any Indians. Although this is Pawnee country and you might even run into some Sioux farther on or maybe some Cheyenne. There was a train through here a couple weeks back that lost a pair of wagons, but we haven't heard of anything since."

"That's good to hear. How's the huntin'? Findin' plenty of game?"

"Not bad, you'll probably run into some buffalo in a day or so, they crossed over the river a couple days back and are probably still hanging around the river bottom."

"Thanks, that's good to know. I'm sure the folks are gettin' ready for some fresh meat and buffalo will sure hit the spot. Well, I gotta get back to them pilgrims, thanks for the info." The scout turned his mount, crossed the river, stopped and waved back at the pair and kicked his horse to a canter to catch up to the lead wagon. Clancy and Caleb dismounted and made a noon camp as they watched the passing of the train. Numbering well over seventy, by the time the last of the wagons were passing, the dust cloud almost obscured them from view. As the dust slowly drifted toward the river, the scum on the water turned the color of the trail as it slowly moved downstream. Caleb observed, "That seems to be the way of it, whenever there's a bunch of people, everything they pass is changed, even the water in the river tells the tale."

"Oh hush, that river is always muddy, it's usually so muddy you can't even drink it. Didn't somebody say it's too thick to drink and too thin to plow?"

Caleb smiled and shook his head at his optimistic but practical wife and reached for another piece of dried deer meat that would challenge the strength of his teeth before he could wash it down with the stiff coffee. After their nooning, Caleb stood to stretch and looked downstream to see a fat buck and doe whitetail tentatively step into the shallows for a drink. With a whisper to Clancy, Caleb slowly reached for his Hawken and leaned against a nearby cottonwood, looked over his shoulder to see Clancy stretched out behind a log with her Hawken pointed downstream and nodded his head for her to take the first shot. The two Hawkens roared with what sounded like one blast as the smoke belched forth the .54 caliber lead balls that brought down both deer. Reloading his rifle as he walked to the downed animals, Caleb searched the surrounding area for any sign of other danger. Clancy remained at the camp and gathered the animals together to join her husband at the task of field dressing the deer.

The mule train made good time and their camp was just upstream from the camp of the hunters. As Caleb and Clancy sat side by side on the log before their fire, they could see the fires of the teamsters less than two hundred yards away. The camp of the train was in a large grove of cottonwood, maple and elm alongside the bank of the river. The wagons made a semi-circle with the river at the back and the protection afforded by the formation was impenetrable. Caleb had told Mac about the Indian sign they crossed and the leader had taken the necessary precautions. The two hunters enjoyed their meal as they shared simple thoughts and enjoyed the night air as the fire burned low before them. Clancy stopped mid-sentence, nudged Caleb with her knee and a slight nod that was answered by Caleb with his own nod and a roll of the eyes toward their rear. A rolled pebble alerted Clancy as he lunged forward and turned mid-air as he reached for his Paterson Colt at his belt. Two men were rushing the pair from behind and Caleb shot once with the smaller of the attackers grabbing at his shoulder but not slowing in their charge. The bigger man grabbed Clancy by the arm and jerked her to her feet and spun her around to face him. Caleb came to his feet to meet the attack of the second man and fired again with the shot taking the attacker plum center and folding him like broken twig. Planting his face in the dirt, the attacker did not move. Caleb turned to see the larger man grasping the upper arms of Clancy and holding her before him to prevent Caleb taking a shot.

"Mister, you better let go of her before I plant you next to your partner here," commanded Caleb as he motioned toward the dead man.

"Ha! You ain't gonna shoot me cuz you'll get yore purty woman here. Now, we didn't mean no harm, we just figgered you'd wanna share her with us. The way you two been struttin' around in front of ever body, we just thot you'd be neighborly, since we ain't got no woman of our own," he snarled with drool dripping from his gaping mouth full of brown stained rotten teeth. His tongue snaked out and licked his lips as he said to Clancy, "Why'nt chu gimme a little kiss you sweet thang you? Huh, just a little 'un?"

Clancy spat in his face and shouted, "Let me go, you vile scum!"

"Scum? I ain't no scum!" he snarled as he released his grip on her arm and cocked back his arm as if to slap her. But in that instant, Clancy grasped the haft on her Bowie and brought it forward and down in a chopping motion that took the side of his face and his entire ear and laid the flesh open on his shoulder clear to the bone. The scream from the man and his released grip brought him to his knees as he grabbed at his severed ear and looked at the woman that dealt the blow. Starting to rise, he reached for her as the Paterson Colt spat flame and the hole through his neck spewed more blood to join that streaming down his chest. The impact of the bullet knocked the man back on his haunches and his eyes bulged as he looked at the venomous stare of the redhead and took the vision of vengeance to Hell with him.

Clancy turned to see Caleb standing with the Colt hanging to his side and the two quickly wrapped each other in a breath robbing embrace. They were standing together entwined when they heard the advancing footsteps of several men approaching their camp. Mac led a group of five armed men that walked into the light expecting trouble. A quick survey by the leader of the mule train told him all he needed to know. Looking at the couple by the firelight he asked, "Are you two all right?" Receiving nods in the affirmative, he continued, "Did what happen here what I think happened? I take it these two tried something they shouldn't?"

"That's right, they came out of the dark and attacked. We just defended ourselves."

"Doesn't surprise me, these two have been trouble the entire trip. After he saw your woman there, he couldn't stop talking about her, but I really didn't think they'd try anything," he said as he walked to the bodies and looked at the damage done to the larger one. "Holy cow! What in the world happened to him, why he's missin' half his face and . . . " as the comment trailed off, he noticed the Bowie knife in Clancy's hand and said, "You did this?"

"That's right," as she held up the knife and looked at it, "I been guttin' and skinnin' the animals you been eatin' on, not much difference one animal or another," as she slipped the knife back into the scabbard behind her shoulders. With another look at the redhead, Mac motioned for his men to drag the bodies away so they could bury them away from the river and with a quiet good bye led his men back to their camp. Caleb heard the men talking as they moved away and one man said, "Boy howdy, she's one woman you don't wanna mess with!"

EARLY AFTERNOON OF THE TWENTY-SIXTH DAY OUT of Ft. John, the mule train crested a slight rise and sighted the settlement sometimes called Council Bluffs after the meeting held there by Lewis and Clark and the Otoe tribe. Caleb remembered coming through here with Jeremiah and Scratch but he remembered a large camp of Pottawatomi Indians across the river and few buildings, most of which were trading posts selling supplies to Western bound emigrants and whiskey to the local Indians. Now there were many buildings and wall tents that spoke of a large number of whites. As he inquired of Mac he was told the town was now called Kanesville and most of the settlers were actually temporary inhabitants, all Mormon, waiting for the opportunity to join a wagon train and go West to their promised land.

Mac continued, "There's even some folks that are starting to call the Oregon Trail the Mormon Trail, cuz there's so many of 'em that are travelin' thataway are them Mormons. Course what a lot of 'em don't know is the

Mormon part of the trail just follers the North bank of the Platte, like we done comin' back, and then it splits off after they cross over South Pass. But who am I to tell all them folks they're just confused."

"Well, as long as they keep goin' after they cross over South Pass that'll be fine with me. I just don't want 'em settlin' in my home country there in the territory, you know, up there in the Wind River Range and such as that," replied Caleb.

Mac pointed to a spot just upstream on the Missouri from the confluence with the Platte and said, "That there dock where that steamboat's tied up, that's where we need to go. I believe that boat's awaitin' on us."

Caleb, Clancy and Mac rode abreast as they dropped down the slight rise of the West bank of the Missouri. A long dock protruded well into the muddy waters of the Missouri and a gleaming white steamboat was tied up but still yawed in the waves of the slow moving river. A wide gangplank led from the dock to the main deck and the dark maw that beckoned. Standing and leaning on the rail of the cabin deck was a well-attired man that waved at Mac and the newly arriving mule train.

"That there's Pierre Chouteau, he's a ram rod or something with American Fur Company and the one takin' delivery on these peltries and hides. He's a good man to know, especially after you get to St. Louie. His family's purty important down there, seems like they own a bunch o' businesses and property and such."

Mac turned his horse back to the train and started shouting orders to the teamsters. Caleb and Clancy dismounted and Clancy held the animals as Caleb approached the boat. A man in a uniform type outfit was walking down the gangplank and Caleb greeted him and reached out to shake hands.

"Howdy. I'm Caleb Thompsett, and that's my wife," he said as he motioned with his head back to Clancy, "we've been guiding for the mule train and we're looking to take the boat on in to St. Louis. You got room for a couple more passengers and a couple horses and a mule?"

"You lookin' to book a cabin or you just wantin' space on the deck," answered the captain as he looked over his spectacles with a careful eye at the young man.

"Well, since I'm travelin' with my wife, I think we'd like to have a cabin if ya' got one?"

"Yes, we have a cabin available, but the fare for each of you will be ten dollars, and for the animals it'll be six dollars each. Course with the animals, you'll have to tend to their feed and water, but whenever we stop for wood, you can take 'em ashore to get a little fresh graze, but only as long as it takes to load the wood, mind you, unless we tie up for the night." His information was delivered as a stern teacher to a delinquent student and it was evident he was skeptical as to Caleb's ability to pay the fare.

"Sound fine," said the young man as he reached into the pouch hanging from his belt and presented the captain with two double eagle twenty-dollar gold pieces. The coins brought an immediate change of attitude to the captain as he said, "Welcome aboard, Caleb was it? And your wife's name?"

"Clancy, but she prefers Mrs. Thompsett," answered Caleb although he didn't think Clancy had ever been called Mrs. Thompsett but he just wanted to poke a little fun at the captain.

"Certainly, certainly," nodded the captain as he turned to the side to make his way past the young man. Passing Clancy, he tipped his cap and said, "Welcome Mrs. Thompsett, I hope you enjoy your trip." Looking first at the passing captain then at her husband, her face told of the confusion and wonder at what just happened. Her answer from Caleb was a back bending belly laugh that elicited a broad smile from his wife.

Six stalls stood empty on the river side of the boat and Caleb and Clancy led their animals to the forward three. The stalls were slightly angled and built of sturdy two by timbers with a hay mow and water trough at the front. Gathering an armload of grass hay for each animal, they filled the mows and taking a bucket, Caleb soon filled the water troughs with river water. The panniers of their supplies were stacked near the stalls and lashed down to the stall sides. The parfleches and saddle bags that held the hidden compartments and bullet pouches of gold were slung over their shoulders and taken to the cabin deck. Directed by one of the cabin hands to their cabin, they soon settled in to what would be their home for the next several days. The cabin was small, about eight feet by eight, a small corner closet and a wash basin on a stand while the sleeping accommodations were two bunk beds against the wall. Two chairs were spaced apart with a small table that held a lamp between. When Clancy saw the bunks, she looked at Caleb and giggled as his expression at the separate beds. The outside of the cabin had a door and one small window, the inside also had a door that opened to the Grand Saloon, or the central area that occupied the space between the two rows of cabins and served as the dining area for the cabin occupants. The parfleches, saddle bags, rifles and other gear were stashed under the beds and in the one small closet next to the water basin. Caleb checked the doors for their sturdiness and locks and was satisfied to their security. He knew their attire and manner would not make anyone think they had anything of great value to be concerned about, but he still chose to be cautious. At Caleb's suggestion, the couple exited to the promenade to walk about the boat and become acquainted with their accommodations.

Their cabin exited on the starboard side of the boat and gave the couple a good view of the activity of the teamsters and workers as they transferred the loads of hides and peltries to the deck of the river boat. Their stroll took them forward and around the front of the cabin deck, noticing the glass front doors that opened to the grand saloon dining area. Continuing their walk to the port side, they leaned on the rail and watched the slow moving waters of the mighty Missouri. With it being late spring, the waters were extraordinarily muddy with the watershed from the far off snow melt in the mountains. Occasionally some debris of drift wood, trees, and even dead animals passed them by only to remind them of the home left behind. A voice from behind startled them with, "Welcome aboard. So, it seems we'll be ship mates for the next couple of weeks." As the couple turned to face their greeter, they noted a well attired distinguished gentleman that was the same that greeted the mule train. Extending his hand, he introduced himself, "I'm Pierre Chouteau from St. Louis. I represent the American Fur Company and that mule train you were with is ours. I understand you worked with them by guiding and hunting for them, is that correct?"

After their handshake, Caleb responded, "Yes, that's right. I'm Caleb Thompsett and this is my wife, Clancy. We traveled with the train from Ft. John and yes we did the hunting and guiding for them."

"Well, then I guess I owe you for your services. Now according to Mr. MacIntosh, you were with them for twenty-six days, and also had eight buffalo hides so at one dollar a day each and eight hides at twelve dollars each that comes to the tidy sum of one hundred forty-eight dollars." As he spoke he withdrew a small pouch and counted out eight twenty-dollar gold pieces and dropped them into Caleb's hand.

"I'm sorry, I don't have the coin to give you the change, which I believe would be twelve dollars," stated Caleb as he looked to his benefactor.

"After Mac explained to me about the trip and your good work as well as the trouble caused to you and your wife, let's just call that even. And I would like to ask you to join me in the grand saloon this evening for dinner. May I look forward to your dining with me?" he inquired as he looked to both Caleb and Clancy.

Without hesitation, Caleb said, "That would be just fine. We'll be glad to join you, and thank you." Chouteau excused himself and the couple resumed their stroll around the promenade of the steamboat. The impressive structure was the St. Ange, owned and captained and piloted by Joseph LaBarge, an experienced and respected captain. The boat was a side wheeler and almost new. This was just the second trip up the Missouri. While commissioned by the Quartermaster's Department for army service, he also had contracted with the American Fur company to make trips to the northernmost fur post of Fort Benton and back to St. Louis. The boat could handle 250 tons of cargo and the cabin deck had cabins and dining on the forward half of the deck while the aft portion was partitioned for cargo. While the larger boats on the Mississippi had the entire cabin deck given to cabins and dining, this was a hybrid between a cargo and passenger vessel. Drawing just four feet of draft, it was very navigable on the Big Mo as the Missouri River was known.

Returning to the starboard side, the couple watched the last of the hides being loaded to the main deck just as dusk settled and the distant plains swallowed the sun. With a cloudless sky, they were robbed of any color for their first evening on the boat, but Caleb assured his wife there would be an ample number of sunsets to view from the deck outside their cabin. Stepping back into their cabin, they washed up and made ready for their dinner with their new acquaintance. "Well, husband, we are definitely going to have to get some new clothes if we're going to be dining with the "gentry" very often. All we have are buckskins, not that there's anything wrong with buckskins, but I think I'd like to try one of those fancy dresses I've heard about and I think you might look pretty handsome in an outfit like what Mr. Chouteau was wearing," she commented with a mischievous smile.

"Of course, you don't think I know that. You'd think I was raised with a bunch of half-naked Indians or something the way you carry on," answered Caleb as he lay on the bunk with his hands behind his head and smiling at his favorite redhead.

She dropped to the edge of his bed and started tickling his ribs, knowing how ticklish he was and the tussle was on, but it only lasted long enough for Caleb to roll her over on the bunk and smother her with kisses, which she enjoyed.

"Now quit it, you big bully you. We've got to get going, or we're gonna miss dinner and I'm hungry!"

THE GRAND SALOON AND DINING ROOM WAS THE central area between the two rows of cabins on the cabin deck. With few passengers on this return trip, there were only four tables with four chairs each spaciously arranged in the large central area. The fore end of the room provided a view of the bow of the boat and the river before them. Although still tied at the dock, the boat slowly rocked to the passing waves of the slow moving Missouri. The interior cabin doors opened to the grand saloon and a few steps brought the couple to the table and their host, Pierre Chouteau. He stood at their approach and as Caleb pulled the chair out for his wife, the captain walked to their table to join them.

"I hope you don't mind, but I've asked the captain to join us," explained Chouteau.

"Of course not," replied Caleb as he finished seating Clancy and turned to extend his hand to the captain. "Captain," said the young man to acknowledge his arrival.

"Mr. Thompsett," then turning to Clancy, "and Mrs.

Thompsett, it's good to see you this evening. I assume you folks have settled into your cabin comfortably?" asked the captain.

"Yes, we have, thank you," replied Caleb as he seated himself.

"I'm glad to have this opportunity to visit with you folks. Is this your first time on a riverboat?" inquired captain LaBarge.

"Yes, it is, we don't have too many river boats back in the mountains and this is one of our few trips away from the tall timber."

"Well, while we wait for our meal, maybe I should give you a little guidance concerning your trip. Especially for your lovely lady, since we don't get very many women travelers, just a couple of precautions to make your time with us a little more enjoyable. First, since you will be taking care of your animals, may I suggest that your wife remain on the cabin deck? You see, the deck crew and many of the deck passengers are not very reputable and would not make good company for a lady. They are a pretty rough crew by necessity, but also not very trust-worthy, Oh, don't get me wrong, they're not a bad bunch but just not suitable for women or to be trusted with your valuables. If you left any valuables with your animals, I suggest you move it to your cabin.

Also, it is not uncommon for some of those on the deck level to come down with Cholera, so if you notice some of those showing signs of sickness, please let me know so they can be tended to promptly. Cholera is another reason to restrict your time on the main deck, it seems to be an affliction primarily suffered by those in less sanitary areas. Also, you will note the two men at the opposite table behind me, they are professional gamblers and not very reputable. However, if you choose to try your luck, remember I warned you. And, if you have any valuables, I do have a safe, not a very large one, in my cabin and you're welcome to put your valuables in it. And finally, on the Lord's day, if we are near a port, we will dock to allow you to attend any church services of your choice. However, if we are not, we will remain tied up for the morning of the Lord's day and we will have services here in the Grand Saloon before resuming our trip downriver. And lastly, if you have not already located them, the privies are just out that door," he motioned with a pointed finger at the door to the starboard promenade deck," for the ladies, and through the opposite door for the gentlemen. Now, do you have any questions for me?" he asked with raised eyebrows as he looked from Caleb to Clancy.

"Yes, Captain, how long will it take us to get to St. Louis?" asked Clancy.

"We'll depart at first light tomorrow and the remainder of the trip will take between two and three weeks at the most and depending on weather, water, and other conditions maybe less."

The cabin boys, three young darkies, had the additional duty of serving the meals to the cabin deck and now appeared from the galley with arms laden with plates of steaming food. As the plates were placed before the diners Clancy noted the aroma and appearance of her first served meal. The centerpiece of the plate was a grilled trout with boiled potatoes to one side and a salad of fresh greens on the other. Another server poured glasses of wine for each one, bowed at the waist and returned to the galley. The Captain was seated with his back to the fore of the boat with Clancy on his left, facing their cabin, Caleb to her left and Chouteau on the Captain's right. The conversation around the table consisted of small talk about life in the mountains compared to the city. Chouteau and the Captain debated travel on the river versus the train and the conversation was foreign to Clancy but she busied herself with the meal and taking in the atmosphere of the Grand Saloon. As her eyes roved from cabin to cabin, she noticed a light coming from under the door to their cabin. She quickly looked at the other cabin doors and saw there was no light from any of those. *Our cabin is facing the West, maybe it's just from the sunset, but no, the door was shut and the window shade pulled and the sun has already set.*

"Caleb, look, there's light coming from our cabin!"

He quickly turned to see what she meant and realizing that someone must be in the room, he jumped to his feet and three long strides took him to the door. Bursting in just in time to see the back of a fleeing man escaping from the opposite door, he quickly glanced around, saw a parfleche pulled from under the bed and the contents scattered, and immediately pursued the fleeing man. Stepping through the open door he looked down the promenade deck both ways and saw no one. He ran to the fore of the boat, leaned over the rail and saw the back of a man disappear below the deck. He had on the same dirty gray shirt as the one that fled the room. He started to leap the rail, and stopped. Returning to his cabin, he lifted the parfleche to the bunk, noted the weight and examined the leather false bottom. Everything was intact except for the few items scattered across the floor. He turned as Clancy stepped through the door, followed by the Captain, and Clancy asked, "What happened? Who was it?" as she looked around at the scattered contents of the parfleche.

"Someone was rifling through our stuff. He must have heard me coming to the door and fled. He jumped over the rail at the front of the boat and dropped to the main deck and disappeared."

"Did you get a good look at him?" asked the Captain with concern showing on his face.

"No, all I could tell was he had on a dirty gray shirt."

"That could be just about anybody, even a member of the crew. Are you missing anything?"

"I don't think so," and then as an afterthought he looked under the bed and in the closet to check on the other parfleche and saddle bags and noted nothing was missing. "I think I surprised him too soon before he could get anything. All he did was pull this out and start rummaging through it. Just a few clothing items, and stuff like that."

The Captain went to the door to check the lock and saw it had been jimmied. "I'll have the steward replace this lock. In the meantime, do you have anything that should go in my safe?"

"No Captain, I don't think so. Whoever it was probably was just looking for anything of value and didn't know mountain men don't have much of value," replied Caleb with a casual smile in the direction of Clancy. She dropped her gaze from his and the action was noticed by the Captain, but he did not address it.

"Well, let's get back to our meal before it gets cold, shall we?" directed the Captain.

Returning to their table, Clancy continued to watch the door to the cabin and Caleb would glance that direction as well. Their nervousness was noted by the Captain, but he thought it was just first time traveling jitters. As they finished their meal, Chouteau pushed his chair back and pulled a pocket watch from his waistcoat, looked at Caleb and began inquiring about his

experiences in the mountains. "So, you lived with the Arapaho did you? How did that come about?"

Caleb began to relate the story of his family in Michigan and the subsequent trip with his Uncle and their friend Scratch. Making the story brief, he soon ended with "And now we're off to see the big city. My Pa said it would be kind of like a belated honeymoon," he said with a smile toward Clancy. He had intentionally left out any reference to the loss of their baby and the grief that prompted the trip.

Pierre Chouteau had listened intently and was evidently thinking about what the young man shared with him. Chouteau was a successful businessman that saw opportunity at every turn of circumstance and was now considering the possibilities of having someone with Caleb's experience in his employ. With his family company that dealt in furs, his partial ownership interest in the American Fur Company, and other businesses, a bright young man such as Caleb might be quite an asset. *I'll have to give this some thought. We've got plenty of time to get better acquainted on this trip and I'll be able to judge his abilities and interest as well. Maybe even his wife could be an asset as well,* thought the businessman as he continued to inquire after the young man's abilities.

Clancy joined the conversation with, "And his name among the Arapaho was He Who Talks with the Wind, because he can mimic the sound of any bird or animal. You should hear some of his bird calls, even they can't tell the difference."

"Really? Well come the morrow while we're going downriver, we'll just have to see what you can do. There are plenty of birds that nest in the trees on the riverbank. That would be interesting to hear," answered Chouteau, more making conversation than expressing any real interest in the birdcalls. As the conversation waned, Caleb pushed his chair back and standing up said, "Well, gentlemen, it has been a long day and I think we will turn in for the evening."

Both the Captain and Chouteau stood as Clancy rose to accompany her husband, and with a slight nod of their heads they said their good nights as the couple walked to their cabin. With the closing of the cabin door, Clancy whispered to her husband, "That man didn't get anything, did he?"

His whispered answer sat her mind at ease as Caleb inspected the door to the Promenade to ensure it was secure. Before they returned to the dining area to finish their meal, he had pushed the dresser against the door and now slid it back in place. Removing the Paterson Colt from the holster at his waist, he put it under the pillow of the lower bunk. His buckskin jacket had obscured the Colt from the view of anyone and he believed the others were not aware of it. As he tucked it under the pillow he said, "That will always be at my side until we have everything safe and secure in the bank in St. Louis. We will have to be very careful and not trust anyone. I don't think the man that was in here found anything, but the weight of the bag with the gold in the bottom would be a giveaway, but I don't think he lifted it. But we still have to be careful. But for now, let's get a good night's sleep. This boat's gonna be movin' in the mornin' and we might want to be on deck to take in the view."

"All this time I never gave a thought to all that gold, but now, just when I was thinkin' we were safe and all, it's gonna be the only thing I can think about," Clancy stated with a bit of a pout.

"Ahh, it'll be alright. I don't think we have anything to worry about," reassured Caleb as much for himself as his wife. "Let's get some sleep, O.K.?"

Rounding the last bend of the Missouri, the St. Ange was bathed in the bright golden rays of the early morning sun. Almost blinding in its brilliance with lances of gold bouncing off the water, the golden orb of morning announced itself with a brilliance becoming the glory of the heavens. Standing at the forward rail of the promenade deck, Clancy basked in the warmth of the sun as she shielded her eyes to see the coming confluence with the mighty Mississippi River. She wore a long tunic of gold tanned buckskin embroidered with intricate beadwork across the front and back yokes. The opening at the neck was loosely laced with leather that dangled its ends across the fringed yoke that was accented by the ivory of elk's teeth. The knee high moccasins topped the fringed leggings that disappeared under the fringed hem of the tunic. Her curly red hair cascaded to the middle of her back and was held away from her face with combs carved and stained from the bone of buffalo.

Caleb paused as he approached to take in the beauty

of his wife. Now bathed in the gold light of early morning, she was the most beautiful image he could ever imagine. With a deep breath and a short sigh, he said, "You are the most magnificent creature God ever made." As she turned to watch him approach, she smiled broadly showing her white teeth and the dimples loaded with freckles and he wished he could capture that image forever.

She turned back to the rail and with a coy smile over her shoulder she said, "Look Wind, have you ever seen so much water?" She would often refer to him by his shortened Indian name in their shared moments together and now pointing forward over the prow of the boat, she motioned to the rapidly approaching confluence of two of the mightiest rivers in the world. The morning brightness temporarily obscured the lesser sights and the visitors gazed at a vista of slow moving water sprinkled with the debris of spring snowmelt and early rains. As they watched, another and larger steamboat, a stern wheeler, thrashed its way through the muddy waters in a race to the St. Louis levee. Pierre Chouteau joined them at the rail and said, "Impressive sight, isn't it?" as he looked from Caleb to Clancy. Caleb noted the admiring glance he gave to Clancy as if he hadn't seen her before. Moving a little closer to his wife, he casually laid his arm across her shoulder and turned to his left to face Chouteau and asked, "Whereabouts is your company located in town?"

Knowing he referred to his family offices and warehouse, the Chouteau Company, Pierre answered, "We're at the corner of Seventh and Chouteau, just take Market Street to Seventh, turn South to Chouteau and we're on the corner. Big building, you can't miss it. Can I expect you in the next day or two?"

Chouteau had spoken extensively to Caleb during the last several days of their trip and had offered the young man employment with his company. His idea was for Caleb to work in the warehouse receiving and grading the furs and talking with the traders and trappers. He wanted Caleb to keep abreast of the fur trapping and the taking of buffalo with his contact with those involved. He had taken a liking to the young man and was impressed with his abilities, experience and intelligence. "I think we can have a very profitable business working together, my young friend and if there is ever anything you need, don't you hesitate. And the same goes for you Clancy, I'm certain my wife and family will be anxious to meet you both. After you folks get your business done in town, we want you to come out to the house for dinner just as soon as you can."

"I'll be looking forward to that, and thank you for telling us about the dress maker and haberdasher. We would have been lost without your help," responded Clancy with a broad smile and a sparkle in her eye. She was anxiously anticipating the days ahead with all the excitement of the big city and the adventure that awaited. Turning back to the rail she sought to take in every sight and sound of the day, watching as the St. Ange made its way into the current of the bigger river and leaned forward in an effort to see even more. Chouteau pointed out different landmarks and as they approached an island, he said, "That's Bloody Island, it got its name from so many duels that were held there and many men lost their lives." The current carried them toward the levee as the Captain searched for an open dock and finding one he masterfully maneuvered the big boat to a gentle nudge of the dock as the lines were thrown to the dock hands to be tied off. The action began with the lowering of the gangplank for the stevedores to begin the task of unloading the many bundles of hides and peltries. Captain LaBarge hurried the workers as the load of cargo for his next trip was waiting at the docks and he was anxious to begin his return trip by early afternoon.

Chouteau said his goodbyes and Caleb and Clancy returned to their cabin to retrieve their belongings. With each carrying a parfleche, a pair of saddlebags, and their rifles in their opposite hands they descended the longer gangplank that extended from the cabin deck to the end of the dock. Walking away from the crew and their unloading, Caleb had Clancy wait with their gear beside a pair of hide bundles and he returned to the boat to get the animals. With all the activity, shouting and noises from the boilers and other nearby boats, the horses were a little skittish but the mule acted as if nothing could bother him. Caleb led the three animals down the gang-plank as the horses nervously watched their footing and the noisy business around them. They were sandwiched between the many stevedores and other workers busy with the unloading. As they carefully made their way down the gangplank, Caleb led the two horses followed by the pack mule on a longer lead and following behind. The mule, although not acting as skittish as the horses, apparently felt crowded by a big black stevedore with a bundle on his shoulder and another one under an arm and without warning kicked back at the man and knocked the bundle from his arm.

"Whoa mule! Boss, I hope youse got a good hold on that there Jack cuz he 'bout took my arm off. I ain't had a scare like dat since I walked behind a pair o'dem in da field"

"Then you shoulda known better'n followin' 'em so close," answered Caleb.

"Yassuh, you right," muttered the big black man as he bent to pick up his bundle. His sweaty muscles rippled in the sunlight as he was shirtless and as he rose to his full height, he said, "An' iffn' you needs a strong hand to work with yo' mule or others, you come see big Reuben."

"I just might do that. Reuben, ya say?"

"Yassuh, been workin' the docks for couple years now and most folks know where ta' find me."

Nodding his head to the big man, Caleb led the animals to the waiting Clancy and prepared to load them with their gear. Mounting up, they looked around at the busy docks and levee searching for a roadway to follow to the Market street Chouteau spoke about. There were more than a hundred riverboats clustered along the five miles of levee in differing stages of loading and unloading. Many just bobbed in the water as decorative corks for the riverfront as they awaited their turn at the docks or the return of their crews to begin a new journey on the river. Cluttering the levee were many stacks of cargo, dray wagons being loaded while the large draft horses left reminders of their visits, men of all colors and manners scurrying in every direction. The noises were a myriad of cacophony with tambourine girls standing and banging their instruments amidst a gathering of fiddlers and organ grinders. To add to the confusion there was a mismatched pair of bagpipers squeezing out songs of the Isles. A variety of opportunists consisting of cigar vendors, girls hocking apples and other fare that stood alongside a gypsy organ grinder and his pet monkey that hustled the passersby with an outstretched cup. There were drunkards and pickpockets and any number and kind of low morale men and women that hustled the new arrivals in any way they could get away with. Adding to the confusion, Clancy noticed what appeared to be homeless ragamuffins snatching crumbs and castoffs from the few lounging workers that sought a brief break from their back breaking work. St. Louis had become a haven for German and Irish immigrants fleeing the poverty of their homelands and now added to the kaleidoscope of cultures and languages found on the waterfront. The mixture of odors from rotting fish, horse manure, sweaty bodies, a myriad of cargoes with their own mystical smells, and the discharge of sewage from the boats and the businesses alike caused Clancy to wrinkle her nose, make a face and hold a hand over her nose and mouth as she said to Caleb, "How do they stand it, everything smells so bad!"

"Well, Pa warned us that we might be missin' the fresh air of the mountains sooner or later, but I didn't think it'd be so soon."

They were following the movement of the masses as carriages, wagons, horses and pedestrians made their way to the top of the levee and the row of white washed business buildings that faced the wharf. Signs, many peeling and illegible, shouted the names or descriptions of the businesses that were hidden behind small glass panes held together to form a display window with further descriptions painted across the distorted glass. Market street was paved with cobblestones and the clatter of the horses' hooves echoed back from the storefronts as Caleb sought to follow directions to the Boatmen's Savings Institution, a bank that Chouteau recommended. Arriving at the front of the bank, Caleb had Clancy wait with the horses and gear until he made the necessary arrangements. Within moments, he returned and the two carried the parfleches and saddlebags into the bank. As Caleb sat the parcels on top of a nearby desk, George Budd rose from his seat and asked, "And just what do you think you're doing?"

"Well, my Pa said we should make a deposit, so that's what we're here for, this is a bank ain't it?"

"Yes, it is, but what is . . . is this?" he asked as he motioned to the pile of parcels cluttering his desk.

"You take gold, don't you?" asked Caleb sincerely.

"Yes, yes of course."

"Then excuse me a minute while I get it out," instructed a smiling mountain man. Taking the miscellaneous items from the first parfleche, he pulled at the corners of the false bottom, lifted it up and began to extract the bags of gold dust that were laying side by side across the bottom of the bag. At the sight of the first bag, the banker's eyes grew large as he reached for the bag and opened its drawstring to examine the contents. He carefully poured a sample of the dust onto his desk pad and whispered, "Oh, my!"

When the last of the bags were emptied and the sizable pile of gold pouches were weighed and tallied, the banker looked at Caleb and Clancy and said, "Young man, this is a considerable amount of money, just what do you want us to do?"

"Well, we're goin' to need to get outfitted and we're gonna need some ready cash so if you would please I'd like some of it in gold coin and the rest we'll leave with you for safekeeping, if that's all right?"

"Of course, of course," he said as he rubbed his hands together in eagerness to fulfill the wishes of his newest and one of the biggest depositors. Caleb had chosen to keep the bullet pouches with the lead covered molded gold musket balls apart from the rest and would use those as reserve funds if needed. As he slid the coins into two of the now empty gold pouches, Caleb asked, "Now, if you could direct us to the nearest livery stable, we would like to have our animals tended to and we have some other business we need to be about."

The horses, mule and tack were welcomed at the Market Street livery and would be gratefully housed and tended by the owner and his stable boy, a youngster that Caleb would later learn, was a homeless waif but a hard worker that loved animals and went by the name of Brewster. The boy immediately proved his worth as he told Caleb and Clancy about the Case and Wells omnibus service, which was essentially a horse drawn cab service for all of St. Louis. "Yessir, all you have to do is flag it down, tell 'em where you want ta' go, and they'll take ya there. Course it'll cost you a couple o' coppers, but it sure beats walkin'" proclaimed the boy.

Caleb had asked the banker for some smaller coins and dropped them into his pocket from which he now drew out a "couple of coppers" for the boy.

"Wow, thanks mister. If I can help ya' with anythin' else, you let me know, O.K.?" To which Caleb gave a nod and a smile as the two burdened visitors began their stroll on the sidewalk en route to the Planters House Hotel. Still clad in buckskins with a saddle bag over his shoulder and a parfleche in one hand and his Hawken in the other, Clancy walked side by side wearing her buckskin tunic and leggings and her Hawken cradled in the crook of her arm. Although mountain men or trappers were not an unusual sight in St. Louis, it was different seeing an attractive redhead white woman attired like an Indian and the two caught many a stare as they walked along the street. Arriving at the hotel on Fourth Street, they entered and approached the front desk under the watchful eye of the desk clerk who wasn't too sure of these new arrivals. After greeting the clerk, Caleb said, "Pierre recommended we put up here and said it was a pretty nice place. Looks pretty fancy, don't you think Clancy?"

"Pierre? Pierre who?" asked the clerk with a suspicious stare.

"Chouteau, surely you know him don't you? We're doin' a little business with him and he said this place would do for us for a while."

With a dramatically changed expression that quickly turned into a condescending smile, the clerk said, "Yessir, yessir. We certainly welcome you to our fine hotel. And how long will you be staying with us?"

"Well, we're not rightly sure. We're meetin' the Chouteau's for dinner tomorrow night and depending on our business, we'll know more then." Clancy turned her head away from her husband as she fought to keep a straight face as she listened to her mountain man act like a real city slicker. They went to their room which was more spacious that either imagined, put their gear on the bed and stood the rifles and accouterments in the corner and started for the door. Clancy asked, "You still have your Colt don't you?"

"Why, of course," replied Caleb as he patted the slight bulge under his jacket at his waist. Then reaching up to pat his wife on the back between her shoulders he said, "And I see you still have your 'toothpick' resting comfortably where you can reach it." To which she nodded and smiled with an "Ummmhummm."

They finished the day with a visit to the haberdasher for Caleb to be fitted for his new city wardrobe and a first visit to the dressmaker for Clancy to start her selection of fashion. At both places, the initial reception was a bit standoffish, but once their wishes were made known and the readiness of their cash, the clerks, tailors, and seamstresses quickly warmed to the prospect of new business. Walking back to the hotel, they chuckled as they talked about their treatment and the subsequent change in attitudes of the salespeople. The excitement of the city was constantly tempered by the rudeness of the people and the stench of the sewage in the streets. Clancy said, "I just don't understand how so many people can be so dirty, and live in such filthy conditions. We never had this in all the years in the mountains with what so many of these people call heathens. They were never this dirty. Even so many of the people smell just like this, like they never bathe themselves. I sure hope it isn't all like this. At least in the hotel, it doesn't smell as bad."

Caleb was unable to respond to his wife's observances as he busied himself with stepping over the sewage filled gutters and around the filth in the street. As they passed a narrow alleyway between buildings, they noticed what appeared as two drunks spread eagled in their own filth and unmoving. The sight prompted them to hasten on their way to the hotel.

THE HOTEL DINING ROOM COULD BE DESCRIBED AS extravagant luxury. The chandeliers radiated the lantern light as the crystals bounced the illumination around the spacious room. Tables were covered with lace edged linen and topped with an array of centerpieces that spoke of the worldly touch of the decorations. Settings of gold edged china, crystal glassware, decorative silverware and linen napkins adorned every table. As Caleb and Clancy were seated by the Maître De, they noticed several curious glances from the other diners. Earlier in their room, Caleb said to Clancy, "I sure am glad that Pa and Scratch gave us some teachin' 'bout the manners and such so we know how we're 'sposed to act around all these fancy folks. If we didn't know 'bout such things, we might just be a bit embarrassed."

"Yes, but the way we're dressed, folks look at us a little strangely anyway," mused Clancy.

"Aw, they're just amazed at how beautiful my wife is

and how good you look with that fine beadwork and such. Or like Pa says, 'they're just jealous.'"

As they were seated, several looked and turned away with whispers to one another. Clancy looked at Caleb and said, "See what I mean? They're so rude!" With a nod of agreement, Caleb focused on the menu and said, "Well, I'm hungry and I don't care what those folks think, come on, let's decide what we want."

As they finished their meal and sat back to enjoy a glass of wine, they were approached by a finely attired young gentleman that fingered his handlebar mustache as he spoke.

"Good evening folks, please allow me to introduce myself. I'm James Heffernan and I couldn't help but notice your attire and I would like to visit with you if I may?"

"Suit yourself, Mister. Glad to have the company. I'm Caleb Thompsett and this is my wife, Clancy," replied Caleb as he motioned to his wife and then to the stranger to have a seat.

"Well sir, the reason for my interest is I'm looking to learn as much about the West as I can and I'm guessing you might have come from out there, am I right?"

"Yes, you're right so far, but why the interest?" inquired Caleb.

"Well, I've been thinking that there might be some good places out West to start a cattle and horse ranch. You know, some place that has plenty of grazing land, not many or any neighbors, and maybe even some wild horses to get a start with."

"Well, there's not too many cattle out there. Lots of

Indians, plenty of buffalo and other wild game, even some wild horse herds, but no cattle. Although there have been some milk cows stray off from a wagon train, but not any cattle."

As the conversation continued over their after dinner wine, Heffernan shared his dream of a large cattle ranch somewhere near the mountains of the Rockies. He also shared that his older widowed sister had the start of a herd in Texas and could provide the starter herd for his dream. As Caleb shared his knowledge of the mountains and plains of the Missouri Territory and his limited knowledge of the adjoining territory of Tejas, the two men came to realize they shared a dream of independence and the possibilities of the West. Vowing to keep in contact with one another, they parted company and Caleb and Clancy returned to their room.

Morning came without fanfare and the breakfast table before them was adorned with plates piled with eggs, biscuits and gravy, bacon and potatoes. Both Caleb and Clancy were surprised at their appetites but didn't hesitate to satisfy their hunger. Their waiter, having enjoyed serving this unusual pair, took time to visit with them and answer some of the usual questions about the city. He went on to caution them about the outbreak of Cholera and said, "A lot of folks think it's in the air, but me, I think it's the water, what with all the sewage and stuff, there just isn't very much good clean water available. Now the hotel here, we have a good deep well, but I don't know for sure. Just you be careful because that Cholera is not to be trifled with." Making plans for the day, they agreed a first visit to the haberdasher and the dressmaker would determine the remaining activities for the day. When the haberdasher told Caleb his attire would not be ready until later in the day, they went next door to the dressmaker. Clancy was greeted with open arms by the matronly dressmaker and she asked for several hours of Clancy's time for fitting and measuring to which Clancy gladly agreed. Caleb excused himself to make a visit to the Chouteau office and warehouse and they agreed to meet back at the dressmaker's for lunch.

The dressmaker and haberdasher were located on Market between fourth and fifth and Caleb walked West on Market as he followed the directions given by Pierre Chouteau. At the corner of Market and Seventh, he hailed an omnibus for a ride down Seventh to Chouteau and the Chouteau Company offices. As he stepped aboard the wagon, he noticed a cloud of smoke at the end of Market street, but just thought it was the combination of so many steamboats firing up their boilers. A short ride brought him to his destination and entering the plain brick two story building, he was greeted by a clerk behind the counter and as Caleb introduced himself, Pierre Chouteau came through a door that had a large pane of glass that bore his name.

"Caleb, glad to see you made it!" and turning to the clerk he said, "This is the man I told you about. Caleb, I'd like you to meet Alexander, our very capable assistant. Alex, this is Caleb Thompsett, he's joining our company and will be working in the warehouse receiving the pelts etc. Caleb, let me show you around."

The tour of the offices was unimpressive, but after the large barn door was pushed open to reveal a massive warehouse, Caleb took a moment to allow his eyes to wander the length and breadth of the high roofed warehouse. Bundles and piles of hides were crowded together throughout the large building and the smell of rotting flesh assaulted his senses. With a team of dray horses, a worker hitched the double tree harness to a large skid that bore a stack of buffalo hides that towered over the worker. With a slap of the leads on the rumps of the team, the horses leaned to their task and pulled the skid to the far end of the warehouse disappearing behind crates and boxes of dry chemicals. As Caleb watched, Pierre explained, "He's taking those hides to the tannery which is in the adjoining building and the source of the worst of the odors. If we didn't have those big double doors to separate them, it would be much worse. Now, over here," he spoke as he directed Caleb to an area of counters that fronted the wide open double barn doors that provided a refreshing flow of air from the street, "will be where you will be working. It is through these doors that all the traders, trappers, etc., bring their hides and peltries. Your job will be to grade them and pay for them, but also to find out as much as you can about the source of the hides and anything else that might be pertinent to our business." He continued to show Caleb around the extensive operation and explain what and how they operated. Caleb was fascinated at the entire business and was eager to learn everything about the business.

One of the last arriving side wheeler steamboats, the White Cloud was moored beside other boats that stood three deep along the levee. A crew member sneaked into one of the cabins, rolled and lit a cigarette as he leaned back to catch a short nap. He was awakened by smoke in the cabin, realized the mattress was on fire and jumped up to drag it to the deck. Stomping on it to put the fire out, he explained to the steward, "I was just passin' by the cabin, saw the smoke and grabbed this hyar mattress to put the fire out." Believing the fire extinguished, he flipped the mattress over and returned it to the cabin, shut the door and returned to his work on the main deck. With the captain and pilot on shore, there was no one on the bridge or on the cabin deck as the workers labored to clean the boilers and prepare for their next trip downriver. No one noticed the smoke or the flames until a crewman from the nearby boat started yelling and pointing, at which time the same crew member looked overhead to see fire licking at the floor boards of the cabin deck. "FIRE, FIRE!" he yelled as he raced for a bucket to fight the fire. As he reached the rail and turned to look up, he realized the fire was beyond control and shouted to the rest of the crew, "ABANDON SHIP! ABANDON SHIP!"

Within moments the entire waterfront was a bedlam of activity with crews shouting, steam whistles screaming, boilers erupting and people yelling with panicked warnings. The White Cloud's moorings were quickly burned through and the burning hulk began to drift with the current, bouncing off nearby boats and spreading the fire indiscriminately. Pillars of smoke became an overlying blanket of black and grey obscuring the sight of individual boats. As the black cloud billowed above the cataclysm, people on shore began sounding the alarm and soon panic set in with bystanders running from the decimation. The crowds pushed and shoved at one another to reach Market street and the avenue to safety.

As the White Cloud spread its holocaust, other boats were carrying this relay of flame further towards the boats nearest the levee and within less than a quarter hour, the flaming debris carried by the winds, soon spread to the clapboard business buildings on the wharf. As the fire sought out more fuel, it crawled along the wooden walkways and soared to the rooftops of the false fronted buildings then leaped from roof to roof as it increased its speed and appetite of destruction. Almost all the boats within reach of the White Cloud shared the consuming flames until it appeared that all the boats at the levee were afire, and with the flames now spreading along the waterfront, there appeared to be no place of escape.

The clang of bells on the volunteer fire department's hose wagons added to the clamor of screaming dock workers and bystanders as they stampeded from the conflagration. Some joined in bucket brigades and the pumpers on the hose wagons worked furiously in vain attempts to stay the advance of the demon. Word was quickly spreading to the usual crowds on the business section streets and workers and customers alike sought escape by joining the throngs fighting for deliverance in the streets.

Pierre and Caleb were just finishing the get acquainted tour when one of the workers ran through the open doors and shouted, "There's a fire on the waterfront! Boats are burnin' and now its spread to the buildings downtown!"

"Clancy! She's at the Dressmaker's! I've got to get her!" exclaimed Caleb as he turned to Pierre. Chouteau quickly responded, "Take my buggy, it's still hitched in front of the office, go! And if you need to, come to our home, it's off thirteenth and Myrtle, by Chouteau pond. Hurry!" Without any hesitation, Caleb ran to the buggy and quickly put the whip to the horse as he turned to head back to the business district off Market street. As he neared the normally busy street, the panicked crowds were pushing one another in their hurry to escape, but the well-trained horse muscled its way through the crowd. Finally reaching the front of the Dressmaker's shop, he saw Clancy and the dressmaker standing in the doorway and watching the crowds push by. At the shout of Caleb, Clancy turned to see him standing in the buggy and yelling at her. She said something to the dressmaker and both women scurried to the buggy to hasten their escape.

With nowhere else to go, Caleb maneuvered the buggy through the now thinning crowds toward the Planter's House hotel. Instructing Clancy to take her friend inside, he led the horse to the rear of the hotel and the nearby stable. Within moments he was at the side of his wife and said, "Let's go to our room, it's high enough up maybe we can get a better view of what's happening."

The destruction they observed was breathtaking in its

enormity. Flames were leaping up to a hundred feet above the rooftops and the monstrous giant would walk from building to building without any hesitation. Brick buildings would be bypassed until the flaming debris would find entrance from a fire enveloped roof and would reach down into the bowels of the building to empty it of any consumable material.

With the fire rushing toward the downtown business district, the firefighters thought the entire town would be consumed until one man, Captain Thomas B. Targee of Missouri Company No. 5, set out a plan of action. As he watched the riverboats be consumed by fire, he noticed that when one would blow up because of the cargo or the boilers, the fire was stayed until it was again spread by other action. This gave the Captain an idea, "Listen men, we need to get as much black powder as we can and then here's what we'll do." He outlined his plan to provide a fire break by blowing up certain buildings in the line of fire in an attempt to save the Cathedral Block and the Market building that housed the city offices, and stop the advance of the fire enabling the different fire companies to extinguish the diminished flames.

As the fire continued its relentless march to the West and North, the fire company under the direction of Captain Targee set the black powder in a line of six buildings. Captain Targee was setting the powder in Phillips Music Store, but before he completed his task, fire licked at the powder and the building was blown up and the Captain with it. The plan was successful as the fire break of six exploded buildings stayed the progress of the fire and as the first light of dawn sought to pierce the black cloud of destruction the flames had met their match and there was nothing left but smoldering piles of rubble. All in all, over 430 buildings had been destroyed and 23 riverboats and over a dozen keelboats and other craft were nothing but ashes. At least three people lost their lives but most thought that number would be greatly increased when the tally of boatmen was added.

Caleb and Clancy and the dressmaker slept very little as they watched the continual march of the fire towards the hotel, but just before they were ready to evacuate, the explosions over a block away from the hotel, stopped the onslaught. Watching the flames turn to nothing more than a bulbous cloud of smoke, they dropped tired bodies into chairs and across the bed to surrender to much needed rest.

THE HOTEL DINING ROOM WAS CROWDED AS CLANCY, Caleb and the dressmaker, Mildred, followed the Maître de to their table. With an overflowing number of guests due to the fire the chatter was livelier than usual with the sharing of experiences and tales abounded. An especially vociferous dialogue rose from a nearby table as a portly gentleman with mutton chop whiskers said, "I'll say it again, I believe the fire was God's own doing and it was because of the spread of Cholera. This fire will purge our community of that dread disease and the filth of the waterfront that promulgated the spread of that contagion."

A long legged slender man that reminded Clancy of a turkey buzzard responded, "But reverend, how can you say such destruction is from God. I don't believe our loving God would resort to such terrible destruction. He could cleanse the community in a much less destructive way, don't you think?" With the contradicting response from his colleague, the portly Reverend lowered his voice but continued his argument. Similar discussions were bantered about among the other diners as they indulged themselves with the sumptuous fare of the famed hotel.

In her innocence and sincere search for the truth, Clancy asked her companions, "Why is it that people are so quick to blame God for the bad but are negligent to give God the credit for so much good that happens?"

"That, my dear, is a question that pious people have repeatedly asked for centuries. I think it's because man wants to take credit for anything good, but they want to blame others for anything bad. It's the nature of man," surmised Mildred.

As they finished their meal Pierre Chouteau approached their table with a brief greeting and a, "I sure am glad to see you folks are all O.K., after you left the warehouse yesterday, I was quite concerned for your safety. As my wife and I discussed the events we agreed that it might be a good idea if you folks were to stay in our guest house, at least for the time being. I'm sure you would find it to be comfortable accommodations and certainly more convenient for you both. My wife would love to have some company as well," he stated as he looked to Clancy, "and I'm sure the two of you would find plenty to keep you occupied." He stood beside Caleb and rested his hand on Caleb's shoulder as he looked at Mildred, "And it's good to see you fared well too Mildred. Is your shop O.K.?"

"I don't know Mr. Chouteau, I'm anxious to find out. These fine folks were going to take me there and if it's all O.K., Mrs. Thompsett and I will continue with her fittings."

"Well, Caleb, I guess that gives you and me time to get started on our business. I'll be in the office but when you get there, please join me and we'll discuss our next move." With a slight bow to the ladies, he excused himself and left the dining room to return to his warehouse. After leaving the ladies at the dress shop, Caleb picked up a parcel from the haberdasher that contained his first set of city clothes but he remained in his buckskins for the day. The morning was spent discussing the business of dealing with the traders and trappers and the possibilities of other sources of the hides and peltries. As Caleb shared with Pierre his knowledge of the Mountains and plains of what would later be called Wyoming Territory but was still known as Missouri territory, he spoke of the Wind River Mountains and the many other mountain ranges both North and South of his mountain home. "There's one area that I haven't spent much time in but my Pa and I hunted there before that I think shows a lot of promise. The mountains aren't as big as the Rockies to the North, but the plains and valleys have a lot more grass and good shelter. It's prime country for buffalo and elk. We've thought about making that area our home."

"And what area is that? It sounds like it would be good country to try doin' some tradin' and maybe even have some hide hunters make a trip out there," replied Chouteau.

As Caleb looked at the response of his benefactor, he pictured results of a large group of hide hunters and the decimated herds and reconsidered his remarks. *The last thing I want is to have a bunch of hide hunters wiping out all the buffalo, especially if we decide to make that our home. And what if James and I want to start a ranch in that area, the last thing we want is a bunch of hide hunters around.* "Well, as I think about it, that might not be such a good area after all, that's right in the heart of Ute country and those folks ain't at all friendly. But you know, the area between there and South Pass has some pretty good country and lots of buffalo and the Cheyenne and Arapaho ain't near as bloody as them Ute. Fact is, they're much easier to trade with and a good trader could probably have a pretty good haul of hides from up there."

"Do you think you'd be interested in leading a brigade of hunters into that area? Maybe help them get a good haul and do a little trading?" asked Chouteau.

"I think I might get 'em pointed in the right direction."

With that thought working in his mind, Pierre looked at his pocket watch, noted the time and looked to Caleb and said, "It's about time for you to fetch your wife. I'll give you a lift over there and then maybe this evening you and your wife can join us for dinner?" Caleb nodded his agreement as he rose to follow Chouteau to the buggy. Upon arriving at the dress shop, Caleb entered to be greeted by his wife attired in a just completed dress and he was surprised at the change in his wife. Not only was she in a full length dress, her hair was put up with curls hanging to the side and a broad smile that spoke of her glee with the response to her attire. With a v-shaped neckline and lace about the neck and collar that matched the lace trim at her wrists, the line of the bodice ended in a point at the waist of the bell shaped skirt. The deep green of the brocade material accented her light complexion and the red curls that fell to her shoulder.

With a deep breath, Caleb said, "You are absolutely stunning, had I met you on the street I don't think I would have recognized you." His broad smile of acceptance and appreciation met with a similar smile from his wife. She turned to Mildred and thanked her, picked up a parcel and handed it to Caleb and said, "I think it's time we returned to the hotel and have a bite to eat, don't you think?"

As they exited the dressmaker's shop, they paused to survey the destruction from the previous night's fire. Workers were busy with the beginnings of the clean-up but their progress was hindered by the overwhelming amount of debris. Smoke still masked the area and the smell of fire and ashes would claim the remnants for months to come. Some crews worked in harmony in their efforts while other remains were picked through by individuals and smaller groups.

The couple stood mesmerized for several moments until Caleb took his wife's elbow and turned toward the hotel. Within a block of the hotel, Caleb walked with his hand cradling the elbow of Clancy as she fussed with the lengthy ties of her small bonnet. A distinguished gentleman frowned as he approached, then stopped before them, tipped his hat and said, "Excuse me ma'am, but is this man bothering you?" as he nodded his head toward the buckskin clad Caleb.

Clancy looked at the man, turned to look at Caleb and back at the man, let a slight giggle escape before she responded, "Why no sir, this is my husband. He has just returned from the wilds of the West and hasn't had an opportunity to change out of his crude attire. But I thank you for your concern sir, you are a true gentleman." Caleb looked at her as if she were crouched mountain lion ready to pounce as the man excused himself and passed them by. Clancy returned her husband's stare, and could hold her laughter no longer. With her head thrown back she let loose with a spate of laughter that would rival a newly freed mule. Bending at the waist, she held her sides as she drew a deep breath to start again, but was stopped by the belligerent stare of her husband. "Crude attire? If you will remember, you're the one that made this 'crude attire' and we both were pretty proud of it then!" Grabbing her elbow, he gave a slight tug and said, "Come on, you shameless hussy, you!"

Clancy continued her giggling for the next several moments until they approached the double doors of the hotel. Then gathering herself, she masked her enjoyment of her husband's embarrassment with a sober and staid expression before they entered the dining room.

As they were being seated, James Heffernan was entering the French doors of the dining room and spotting the couple, moved to the side of their table. "Mr. and Mrs. Thompsett, may I be so bold as to ask if I may join you?"

Caleb was pleased at the arrival of his new-found friend and gladly motioned for him to join them for the meal. After Clancy was seated, the men seated themselves and the conversation quickly turned once again to the future plans of Heffernan. The preliminaries of the discussion were interrupted by the waiter to take their order. Caleb ordered for both himself and Clancy and couldn't help noticing the surreptitious glances from

James toward Clancy and Clancy's slightly embarrassed responding but demure smiles. The waiter turned away as James focused his attention on Caleb and said, "After visiting with you the other day, my mind has been racing with the many possibilities of the area you spoke of for a possible ranch. Where exactly was this veritable paradise for livestock?"

"Well the area that I believe would be most suitable was in the Medicine Bow range. There is a wide valley there, probably twenty or more miles across between that range and the taller mountains of the Rockies just West of there. Although there's a lot of buffalo and elk that make their home there, I think it would support a pretty good size herd of cattle."

"My sister and her new husband have a pretty good size ranch down in Texas country and the last time I visited her, we spoke of the possibility of having another operation up North and I think that area you're speaking of would be just right. We, my sister and I and of course her husband, would provide the cattle and if you would be willing to locate the place and set up, we could do a drive of say, a thousand head, to get a good start up there. What do you think?" asked James as he glanced from Caleb to Clancy and back again.

His roving eye was not missed by Caleb, but he put it off as a curious glance at a beautiful woman that just happened to be his wife. To answer the question, Caleb said, "Well, it's certainly something to think about. We really haven't decided where we want to put down roots, but what you say definitely sounds interesting. Let me give it some thought and we'll keep in touch." The conversation once again turned to the Irishman's curiosity about the West and the many adventures had by his new found friends. When James discovered that Clancy was also from Kilkenny, Ireland, the conversation became one of common ground between the red head and the would-be rancher Irishman. Although Clancy was very young when her family left Ireland, she enjoyed listening to James talk about their home country and Caleb was excluded from the conversation and none too happy for it.

As the conversation subsided, a bellman approached the table, bowed and extended a note to Caleb. As he looked it over, he turned to Clancy and said, "It's from Pierre, he asks that we come to his house for dinner this evening and also says to bring all of our personals and plan on staying in their guest house," he announced with a broad smile.

"If that's Pierre Chouteau you're referring to, that's great. My brother and I have also received a dinner invitation, so perhaps we'll see you both this evening then?" spoke James.

He rose from the table, offered a handshake to Caleb then turning to Clancy as she lifted her hand he bowed and kissed the back of her hand with an "Until this evening then." He turned quickly and walked off before anything else could be said. Caleb stared at his retreating back and was somewhat surprised at the mix of emotions that welled within him.

WITH SALT AND PEPPER CLOSE CROPPED HAIR AND A well-trimmed white beard, the liveried negro called at the desk for the Thompsetts. They were just descending the stairs and presented a picture of the fine gentleman and his wife. Wearing a striped ascot in a broad but lazy bow around his high collar, the white shirt was prominent from his rounded chest waistcoat of tan wool. A dark brown frock coat flared away from his striped trousers and he carried a broad brimmed tan flat crowned hat in his right hand at his side. With a crooked arm, he escorted his wife still attired in her dark green brocade gown that was now topped with a lace shawl that fell carelessly off her right shoulder. As Caleb slipped a finger under his collar in a vain attempt to relieve some of his discomfort, he looked at his wife with pride and held his head high as he escorted her to the waiting carriage. The driver stepped to his seat and with a cluck of his tongue the matched pair of dapple grey horses leaned to their task.

The short jaunt to the Chouteau's soon brought the

carriage alongside the stone wall that surrounded the central portion of the estate. Their view from the carriage revealed most of the two and a half storied home. The impressive mansion of brick had a first floor veranda set off by stone pillars and a second floor covered balcony with wooden pillars and a waist high balustrade. The hip roof was accented by two dormers that spoke of rooms or attic on the third floor. A large chimney protruded from the center of the roof and another larger chimney stood sentinel at the far end of the massive structure. Stopping before the short stairway that led to the veranda and the double-door entry, the driver told the couple he would take their belongings to the guest house and their new home would be tended to by a house-maid named Penny. Caleb thanked the driver and assisted his wife as she descended from the carriage and looked up at the mansion with wide eyes that glowed with her excitement.

"Welcome, welcome," came a light but sincere voice from a petite woman standing to the side of Pierre. She was simply attired in a rose colored gown not unlike that of Clancy. Her neckline was scooped with a trim of erect lace that accented the white complexion of the tiny woman. Her hair was parted in the middle with several long black curls holding a dusting of grey hanging on each side to frame her face with a petite nose and bright shining dark eyes. A smile painted her face with an expression that echoed her words of welcome and she stretched out her arms to give a welcome hug to Clancy. Although Clancy was a full head taller than the petite woman, Emile took the red head's arm in hand and steered the young woman into the welcoming home. As the women disappeared into a sun room that was adjacent to the kitchen, the men strolled the veranda as the Chouteau's awaited their other guests.

With the guests late in arriving, the stroll of the men turned into the home as Pierre continued his guest tour. Several paintings adorned the halls as Pierre explained, "That distinguished gentleman is my grandfather and founder of St. Louis, Rene Auguste Chouteau. The lady in the portrait beside that is of my Great Grandmother and matriarch of the family, Marie-Therese Bourgeois Chouteau. The artist just finished a portrait of my father, Jean Pierre, and it will hang alongside these. However, my father refuses to allow it while he still lives, he says this is 'the hall of the dead' and he's not dead yet!" The comment elicited a chuckle from Caleb as he remembered a similar attitude from his adopted grandfather, Black Kettle, before he died when they traveled to the Medicine Wheel.

A hail from the front door announced the arrival of the other guests, the brothers Heffernan. Caleb and Pierre joined them in the entryway and the dinner was soon announced. With the women joining them, the group was seated around a long rectangular table that was set for seven with the patriarch, Jean Pierre, at the head of the table. Pierre and Emile and John Heffernan were to the patriarch's right and Caleb, Clancy and John Heffernan on the left. Although Jean Pierre was ninety-one years old, he was still of sharp mind and quick wit as he commandeered the conversation. "So, Mr. Thompsett, my son tells me you were raised among the Arapaho in the Territory and your wife as well, that must be a very interesting story. Would you mind sharing it?"

"Well, it's not all that interesting, just a little different than most. But it began when my mother fell ill and my Uncle Jeremiah came to call and . . . " as Caleb wove the tale of his journey West and the subsequent years with the Arapaho and the rescue of Clancy, all were held in rapt attention to the years in the wilderness. As he concluded he said, ". . . and so we decided to make this trip kind of as a belated honeymoon, as my Pa described it."

"Interesting, interesting, and my family has had its share of time with the Indians as well. As a matter of fact, Pierre there started trade with the Osage tribe before he turned sixteen. And there have been many forays into the West, establishing trading forts and such, among the Sioux, Cheyenne and even the Blackfoot. I don't believe we've had any contact with the Arapaho though. Have we son?" he asked as he turned to Pierre.

"No father, we have not had the opportunity to trade with the Arapaho, and several other tribes for that matter. "

Emile interjected herself into the conversation as she asked James Heffernan, "Tell me, Mr. Heffernan, has there been much of the epidemic Cholera where you've been?"

"Not of an epidemic scale, ma'am, but there seems to be no place that is safe from that dread disease," answered James. John joined the conversation with, "And from what I hear, this year's epidemic here in St. Louis is the worst ever."

"We overheard a reverend at the hotel declare that the fire was a judgment of God and was sent to cleanse the city of the epidemic," shared Clancy.

"But as I understand it, my dear, the epidemic continues to grow. Dr. McPheeters believes it's because of the foul air in the city. We have several friends that are considering leaving the city, going to their country estates, until after the epidemic passes. At least they would have fresh air to breathe," exclaimed Emile.

"I don't think that's necessary. We have clear air right where we are. The large pond provides plenty of water, trees, and all that's necessary for a pleasant environment. Besides, we have a deep well for the house and the guest house, and if we need extra water, the cistern provides all we need. I know it has been rumored the pond has become a common place for the refuse carts to dump their waste, but that pond is big enough to handle it, and I'm sure the constabulary will soon stop the dumping. Besides, that waste provides food for some of those creatures and bottom feeding fish, you know, catfish and the like," proclaimed the patriarch. "But for now, if you will excuse me, this old man must retire."

The parting of Jean Pierre was the start of the exit of the guests and for Caleb and Clancy to make their way to the guest house. Greeted at the door by the maid, Penny, they were pleasantly surprised at the spacious cabin that reminded them of their log home in the mountains. With only two rooms, one being the bedroom and the larger furnished with a small dining table and chairs, a kitchen counter with one of the new-fangled hand pumps for water, and two comfortable chairs facing the fireplace, the couple thought they would be very comfortable in this temporary home. Penny had put their personal things in the bedroom, hung the rifles on the provided pegs above the fireplace mantle with the possibles bags and powder horns hanging from a peg beside the fireplace. All in all, they felt right at home. After Penny inquired about any other needs, she dismissed herself and said she would be back in the morning to tend to the fire and anything else they needed.

"Tomorrow I'll bring the horses and mule out, Pierre said to put them in the stable by the barn. With the horses here, we'll be able to go for a ride and view the entire estate."

"I'd like that. But I certainly enjoy visiting with Emile, she is wonderful, kinda like having another Ma," surmised Clancy as she struggled to get out of her layers of new clothes.

"I know what you mean, although he doesn't treat me like that but Pierre is a bit like Pa with his curiosity and helpful ways. I like 'em both," and as he fought buttons on his waistcoat, "but I'm not sure I'm likin' these duds." Clancy smiled and they both started a giggle session as he lifted her in his arms and started to the bedroom.

Two weeks after the fire and little had changed. Although most of the streets had been partially cleared, the debris and destruction still scarred the once valiant city. The smell of charcoal and ashes blended with the usual stench of the downtown area that reeked with the myriad of odors of sewage, tanneries, graveyards, slaughterhouses and stables and did nothing to allay the fears of the people. Many had accepted the theory of Dr. McPheeters that it was the foul air and noxious fumes that spread the disease of Cholera. This was called the miasma theory, and it was this theory that finally prompted the leaders of the community to take action.

After Clancy witnessed the poor sanitary conditions of the city and compared what she saw with the lifestyle of the Indians, she refused to drink any of the water that was made available. Recalling the practice of the Indians whenever they established a new location for the village or any camp, it was understood by all that the only water to be consumed would come from well upstream from any animals or chosen places for relief of bodily functions. Never would anyone bathe or use any water that was below the camp but all willingly made the trek well upstream to gather any water for drinking or cooking. She didn't understand why something that was so easily understood was not practiced by these many people of the city. She was even careful about the water drawn from the well-pump in their cabin. She would smell it, taste it, and even let it run through her fingers and if there was any doubt about it, she would boil it in a pot on the stove before using it. She had discussed this with Emile and the older woman assured her, "Oh my dear, we've had Cholera visit the city before but we've never had any problems. I believe it is a disease of the poor, you know, those that live in the poor neighborhoods in their shanties and those on the riverboats, the crew and others. We don't have to worry about it. Even though many of our friends have left for their country homes, we'll be all right dearie."

When she visited Mildred the dressmaker for additional fittings and clothing, the two women would often discuss at length the problems with the city. With many of the prominent women of the city using her services, Mildred was privy to several normally private conversations between the women and their husbands. While measuring Clancy for a new dress, Mildred suddenly exclaimed, "See, there it goes again," pointing out the window at a passing high sided wagon, "that's another of those terrible refuse wagons. They say they're picking up as many as seventy bodies every day. They go to the hospitals and just drive around town and pick up the bodies. It's terrible, I say, terrible. And they say they don't even get all the bodies, oftentimes the families just bury 'em wherever or even throw the bodies in the river. Poor souls, whatever is this city coming to?"

"You mean that one wagon picks up that many bodies every day?" asked Clancy.

"Oh no dear, there are several wagons, and did you know they have made it a law that the steamboats coming upriver have to put any infected people out on Arsenal Island or they won't be allowed to dock? I don't know if that'll do any good, but at least they're trying to do something," declared the dressmaker.

The spread and toll of the disease seemed to capitalize most conversations in all quarters of the city. When Caleb entered the tannery portion of the warehouse, he held a patch of cheesecloth to his nose and listened as his guide spoke, "Yessir, it do stink in here, shore enuff, but I don't agree with what most folks is sayin' and that is that the smells of the city is what's makin' the Cholera spread. I been workin' here in this tannery for most of ten years and the Cholera has come and gone and I ain't never got it.

'Now see that big vat there? That's just the cleanin' vat. Ain't nuthin' in there but water, gittin' the salt and stuff offn' them thar hides and kinda softens 'em up a mite." As they continued walking, the worker, Zeke, pointed to the broad sturdy tables and the workers pounding the hides with large wooden mallets and continued, "They're softenin' 'em up a mite and the scrapers there're cleaning off any flesh and fat left, and that next vat's where we remove the hair." Caleb got a whiff of the next vat, looked at the guide and said, "Is that? . . . "

Zeke chuckled a bit and said, "Shore is! See we got us a tank wagon that goes on a reg'lar route to the hotel, boardin' houses, even the hospital. They dump them chamber pots in thar and we use it to take the hair off. Boy iffn' them rich folks knew what they're stuff was doin' they'd probly' wanna charge us fer it. You know them rich folks think even their waste water's bettern' everbody' else's."

Passing the hair vat, another set of tables and workers busied themselves scraping hides to remove any excess hair. Another large vat, easily six-foot-high and ten feet in diameter, the same size as the others had another distinct odor emanating from it which Zeke explained was from the Tannins, the chemical that came from animal brains and from the bark of some common trees like the oak. The combination of odors and stench from the putrefying hides was almost too much for Caleb and as Zeke noticed his charge becoming quite pale, he led him out of the building through a large sliding barn door. The sudden whiff of what seemed to be fresh air brought Caleb around and he soon realized the air outside wasn't much better than that inside. As he thought about the tanning process used he asked Zeke, "And what do you do with the contents of the vats after they've lost their effectiveness?"

"Oh about onct' a month, we haul the waste out and dump it either in the river or in that big pond yonder," pointing in the direction of Chouteau's pond.

"But isn't that where the city gets its water?" asked a bewildered Caleb.

"Well yeah, but we dump it clear at the upper end and by the time the water gets down there where it goes to the city, why it's all mixed in and settled and it won't do no harm."

Caleb just shook his head at this revelation and made his excuses to his guide and started his return to the warehouse and his place at the counter. While he walked he thought of the many times he watched the Indians tanning their hides with much less work, little or no odors, and much better results. *It seems like the white man does his best to complicate everything he touches* he thought as he stepped behind the counter.

A blatant reminder of the failure of the city doing little to address the growing problem of sewage was Kayser's Lake in the northern part of the city. An engineer named Henry Kayser had an idea he presented to the city, to use the limestone sinkholes beneath the city as a natural sewer. Surprisingly, this worked until some heavy rains came in late May and the sewage backed up and formed a large pond of wastewater which garnered the name of Kayser's Lake. As the plague continued its rampage, several prominent citizens sought to take things into their own hands, among them Pierre Chouteau. The citizens chose to meet without any of the city officials except the mayor and after lengthy discussion initiated several steps to try to clean up the city. Among them, and at the suggestion of Pierre, hogs were no longer allowed in the city and the refuse pick up had to be improved. Other steps taken were to ban any fish taken from the river and vegetables were banned from the city markets. Even beer was banned for the remainder of the summer.

After almost a month of these processes, Pierre told Caleb, "I think these steps might be working, although it doesn't seem the death toll has diminished any."

"Well, maybe not, but I think the stench is not quite as bad, but then again, I might just be getting used to it. Clancy has talked about maybe trying to help at the hospitals, she thinks there are some native remedies that might help. What do you think? Should she help out? I'm not really sure it'd be safe, but she's getting a bit restless sittin' at home."

"You know, the wife was thinking about getting out and maybe taking in that new play at the theater. Why don't you and your wife join us, it's tomorrow night, and maybe we can all discuss that 'helping out' together," invited Pierre.

Caleb smiled as he continued, "I think that'd be fine. She has a new dress that she was wantin' to show off and that just might be what she needs. Sure, we'll be happy to join you."

The evening of the theater outing, Clancy was invited to the main house to join Emile for the ladies to get ready for the big night out. After almost two hours of talking, primping, and adjusting, the ladies came down the stairway one after another. Clancy led the way as Caleb and Pierre waited in the entryway for the antici-pated arrival of the ladies. Adorned in a pink silk moiré gown with a scoop neckline that was accented by a black silk ribbon holding a cameo given her by Emile, Clancy's smile illuminated the entry. The fitted bodice of the gown sported short sleeves and came to a point at the front of her waist. The tiny pleats around the waistline made the bell shaped skirt blossom and drape to the floor where the floral border of the skirt accented the overall effect. She was followed by Emile looking very aristocratic with a pale green gown with a similar cut as Clancy's but trimmed in a dark green silk ribbon at the waist and sleeves. Distinguished with her silver tipped hair falling in curls at the side of her face, she sought to yield all attention to her younger companion. Both men smiled broadly as their ladies approached them and offered the men their lace wraps to allow them to assist in draping them over their shoulders. Both men wore pleated trousers and waistcoats with dark frock coats cut to mid-thigh. Their loosely tied ascots gave both a careless but distinguished air.

Offering his arm, Pierre set the example as he said, "Ma'am, will you join me for a night at the theater?" Emile quickly stepped to his side as they led the way across the veranda to the waiting carriage. Caleb and Clancy followed as they smiled and laughed together and entered the horse drawn conveyance. Upon arrival at the theater, they were escorted to their box to take their seats just in time for the opening curtain. The play was a new comedy *Box and Cox* about two men that have rented the same flat from a less than honorable lodging-house keeper and upon discovery confront the woman to her dismay. After further conflict and a pending duel, the men also find out they have been engaged to the same woman and are now in peril of being unwillingly wed to her, but circumstances lead her to another, a Mr. Knox. The play was enjoyed by all and after much wiping of tears from continual laughter, they soon depart for home. But all the discussion about the evening and the play forestalled any discussion about Clancy helping at the hospital and the couple soon retired without resolving this very important question.

The following morning a brief discussion during breakfast at the Chouteau mansion followed by intercession from Emile, Caleb condescended to Clancy trying her native remedies with Dr. McPheeters permission, on some of the patients at the hospital. However, Emile insisted on accompanying her young charge on this mission of mercy.

THE LITTER OF CURIOUS AND RAMBUNCTIOUS puppies swarmed around the feet of Caleb and Clancy as they stepped onto the veranda. The large crate that had been their home was overturned and the eleven puppies scampered helter-skelter the breadth of the veranda, paused with a curious look at the steps leading to the yard, and with the bouncing capers of newly weaned pups, returned to the feet of the laughing couple. Bending over to pick up one chubby fur ball that refused to leave her feet, Clancy lifted him to her chest and rubbed her cheek against his. With a flashing red tongue that darted from his black bundle of fur, the flashing eyes of curiosity caught those of the young woman and love blossomed. "Doesn't he remind you of Two Bits?" asked Clancy, referring to her longtime companion that stayed behind in the mountains to live out his old age with Jeremiah and Laughing Waters, her adopted parents. The big dog had aged to the point that a long trip across country would have been too much and the family thought it best for him to remain behind and enjoy his sunset years in leisure.

Reaching out a hand to pet the head and rub the ears of the wiggling pup, Caleb replied, "Yeah, he does, and judging from the size of his mama, he'll grow up to be about as big as Two Bits," then looking at his beloved he smiled and continued, ". . . but your big heart is gonna get you in trouble. You can't adopt a whole litter, why there's almost a dozen here. And if you only want one, howya gonna choose?" Knowing by her expression it was already decided she would have a puppy and it was not open for discussion.

"I don't have to," she drawled, ". . .he chose me! And what do you mean my big heart is gonna get me in trouble?"

"Well, you know, this hospital thing. I'm still not comfortable with you goin' down there with all this Cholera stuff goin' on. I just don't want anything to happen to you. Clancy, when I thought I lost you when you were taken by those men back in the mountains, I thought my world had come to an end. I didn't think I could go on without you, and I still don't," explained Caleb with frustration showing on his face and in his stance.

"Wind, don't you understand? When we lost our baby, I felt helpless and useless. There was nothing I could do and I just wanted to scream and more, but now, there's a chance I might be able to help someone else and I need to at least try. Maybe I won't do any good, but please let me try. With all this crazy stuff happening, the fire and epidemic, it just seems like there's nothing but death everywhere. And it's been so long since we could see past the next building or street and breathe fresh air, we can't even go for a ride and see anything but remnants of the fire or more filth, I'm sick of it but I've got to try to do something," answered the redhead as she stomped her foot on the planks of the veranda with determination and frustration.

"Sounds to me like you're gettin' as tired of the city as I am, are you sayin' you're ready to go back to the mountains?"

The big green eyes of the woman searched those of her husband and a smile began to stretch her lips to reach her dimples. Caleb thought *those smiles have been few and far between.*

"Maybe," she whispered a little flippantly then kissed him with a quick peck on the lips and turned back to the door with the pup still cradled in her arms.

Clancy's idle days at the Chouteau estate were often spent with short rides around the estate grounds to exercise her appaloosa and to give Clancy a change of scenery. As had become her habit since the beginning of her tutelage by her adopted Ma, Laughing Waters, she watched for plants that could be used for medicinal remedies. The rides yielded a plentiful harvest that soon had her shoulder bag straining with leaves, roots and berries. Sometimes these were used for cooking, but as often as not, they were dried or ground up to a powder to replenish her supply for medicinal applications. It was this shoulder bag of remedies that she carried into the hospital at the side of Emile as they searched for Dr. McPheeters.

"Dr. McPheeters," exclaimed Emile as she spotted her longtime friend and physician stepping in the side door. He lifted his head and upon seeing the two ladies, he forced a smile and a greeting. "Why Mrs. Chouteau, what brings you here. Surely you haven't been taken by this disease?" he asked as he waved a hand to indicate the many patients on cots and pallets that crowded the long room. Sunlight was filtered through opaque curtains and large windows to reveal a room that did more to resemble a warehouse than a hospital. Both women held hankies to their nose and mouth to filter the stale air and the stench of excrement, vomit, and death. The doctor walked to the waiting ladies and directed them into a small side room.

"Now ladies, to what do I owe the pleasure of your visit?" asked the doctor. His hair was ruffled, the suspenders of his trousers fought to fulfill their assigned task as they stretched over his ample paunch, with rolled up sleeves and oval shaped reading glasses loosely perched on his nose, he examined the visitors as he would an unwelcome inspector.

"Well, Doctor, we are here to see if we may be of assistance to you. This," pointing at her young companion, ". . . is the wife of a close friend and she of course is a dear friend herself, Mrs. Clancy Thompsett. Mrs. Thompsett has considerable knowledge in natural remedies gained from years spent with the natives in the wilds of the West, and she thought perhaps these remedies might be helpful to you," explained Emile with her usual dignified but friendly manner.

The doctor looked from one to the other of his visitors and shook his head. He knew their offer to help was well intentioned but was based on either a lack of information or simple misunderstanding. "Ladies, I thank you for your kind offer and yes, we are dreadfully understaffed and all help would be welcome, but there are several things you need to understand. First, the average stay of a typical volunteer is less than a day. What with the conditions of the hospital, the terrible conditions and consequences of the disease and the overwhelming miasma of the location, most volunteers succumb to either their own weaknesses or sometimes to contracting the disease.

You see, I'm of the opinion, as are many of my associates, that this disease is a direct result of the terrible conditions of the very air we breathe. The stench of the sewage, the tanneries, the slaughterhouses, the stables and the rot of the waterfront, to mention a few, seem to combine to pollute the very air we breathe and our bodies react violently and Cholera does its foul deed on our weakened bodies." The women looked at one another and again at the doctor as he continued.

"Let me explain to you the way this disease manifests itself. First, it starts with nausea that is not unlike any other time one would experience an upset stomach. Then it swiftly increases in intensity with the patient vomiting freely and profuse and frequent expulsion from the bowels, at first quite bilious in character. Soon it becomes pure 'rice water', or looking like the milky water that has small pieces of rice. Then they are afflicted with severe abdominal pain and their skin starts to turn a blue color and they become wrinkled and looking like death warmed over. Often within hours they succumb. All the while, everything about them and around them takes on the stench of the vomit and defecation and ultimately death itself."

The women fought to keep from regurgitating as the images made vivid in their minds implored their entrails to empty themselves. Holding their hankies tight against their mouths and noses, their complexion displayed a much paler color. Caleb steeled herself and asked the doctor, "How long does all this take to happen, before the patient 'succumbs' as you put it?"

"Oftentimes it is not more than a day from the first symptoms until death," he declared soberly. *I'm tired of these do-gooders trying to salve their consciences with nothing but good intentions and placating words. I wish they'd just leave me to my work and stop wasting my time.*

"But doctor, do you think it possible that some of these remedies that have worked for generations among the Indians, might be of some use? Surely it's worth a try?" asked the hopeful Clancy.

"The problem as I see it, Mrs. Thompsett, is that once a patient is afflicted with Cholera, they have absolutely no interest in taking anything, food, medicine, even water. So, it would be difficult at best, and more than likely impossible to administer any of your remedies."

Emile interjected, "Clancy, why don't you leave some of your remedies with the good doctor, tell him how they are to be used, and perhaps he or his helpers might be able to give them a try," then turning to the doctor she asked, "Would that be acceptable, Dr. McPheeters?"

Seeing a way to end the visit he quickly responded, "Why yes, Mrs. Chouteau, that would undoubtedly be the most efficient manner for these remedies to be put to use. I would be glad to try them at the first opportunity."

Clancy recognized the conspiratorial tone of doctor and her friend, but realized there would be no other means to offer any additional help. Looking from the doctor and back to her friend, she reached into her bag and withdrew several different packages, explained each one to the doctor beginning with the tea made from the inner bark of the chokecherry to the powdered root of Sheep Sorrel and several others. Then standing and excusing herself, she started for the door and was quickly followed by Emile. As they exited the hospital building and approached the waiting buggy, Emile said, "Well my dear, I think we've done all we can. We should count ourselves fortunate that we will not be subjected to such a dread disease."

"Well, maybe so, but I just wanted to be of help in some way. Maybe the doctor will actually try some of those proven remedies, but I don't really think he believes any of them will help. Maybe not, but I know they have worked against what the villagers called the runs, but I'm sure this Cholera is much worse than that," she surmised as she climbed into the buggy after Emile.

Most businesses in the city either had their own or had access to a nearby stable to accommodate their workers and the Chouteau Company had an especially commodious stable. Accommodating the horses and buggies used by the workers and the draft horses utilized in the business itself, the company stable and corrals were unusually large. As Caleb dropped from his saddle, he led his appaloosa into the corral, removed the tack and placed that saddle on the top rail of the corral fence and the bridle and saddle blanket atop the saddle. As he entered the large doors of the warehouse and receiving counter, he saw Pierre pouring himself a cup of coffee from the large enamel pot that sat on the potbellied stove behind the counter. Caleb greeted his friend, poured himself a cup, hopped upon the counter and asked, "Have you decided about the hunting brigade that you suggested I lead to the mountains?"

"Actually I was just thinking about that and wanted to discuss it with you. Have you got a few moments?" inquired Pierre.

Caleb glanced around, leaned to look out the receiving doors, and said, "It looks like I've got plenty of time. It's been a few days since we've received any hides and it sure doesn't look like they're standing in line this morning either."

"First, I'd like to hear from you and what you think the prospects are for a successful hunt and trading expedition to the plains area West of Fort John," proclaimed Chouteau.

"Let me be totally honest with you Pierre. You've become a very good friend and since we've been here you've almost been like another father, so I want you to know everything. First, Clancy and I are quickly becoming dismayed with the city and are seriously considering a return to the mountains. Now that would work out very well for leading the brigade and mule train to that part of the country, but we would not be returning with it. I'm thinking we've had enough of the city and probably won't ever leave the mountains again. However, it would not be difficult for those on the mule train to return the same way and wouldn't necessarily need a guide to get home. Knowing that, if you still would want me to take a brigade out and get them started on their hunt, do a little trading with the different tribes on the way, then I'll do the very best I can. It's the least I can do for all the kindness and friendship you've shown us."

With a broad smile, Pierre stepped to Caleb's side, extended his hand for a handshake and said, "That's exactly what I wanted to hear. It was pretty evident you were becoming a little restless, but I think what you proposed is exactly what we need. I don't think it will be hard to get a brigade together, but I think you might be challenged by one other factor. I don't know if you've heard, but there's the start of quite a gold rush to California territory, they're calling the dreamers 'the 49ers', and you might have a hard time keeping your hunters and other workers of the brigade together. But, that's a different problem to be dealt with if and when it becomes a factor, for now, we need to start making preparations for this trading and hunting venture!"

AFTER THE REBUFF FROM THE DOCTOR, THE NEWS from Caleb was happily received as Clancy embraced her husband and asked, "Does this mean we can leave this cesspool of a city?"

"Absolutely! Pierre said we can start making the preparations tomorrow and there will be a lot to do. I'll have to find enough men and equipment so we can get started as soon as possible, but I don't think it'll take too long, we might even be on the way within a month or less!" he answered enthusiastically. The couple continued their chatter well into the night as they excitedly shared their joy and anticipation of returning to the mountains.

Morning came with a knock on the door from the house-maid Penny as she shared an invitation from the "big house" for the couple to join the Chouteau's for breakfast. While sharing the meal, the men discussed the necessary preparations and time frame for the departure of the brigade. When asked about recruiting the needed men, Pierre shared, "I think the best place to start is the many taverns and mercantiles on the waterfront. Most of the trappers and other men of their interest could be found somewhere down there. There are several of the taverns that have rooms to let and those places usually have riverboat crews, muleskinners, trappers and others that might be interested in a hunting brigade."

"What about wagons and mule teams? Where should I begin looking for them?"

"As far as wagons go, we have three or four at the warehouse that would be good and we have a few mules, but you'll need to check the many liveries around for more and maybe some of the nearby farms. I've sent word by Captain LaBarge to Independence to a well-known wagon maker and he's making up another dozen wagons that will be waiting for you. You'll take the wagons we have for your supplies until you get to Independence, and you'll have plenty of mules to get there, too many to try to send up on a riverboat. So, you'll need to get enough men to handle the mules and horses you get, plus any you pick up from the nearby farms. So, the men will have to do double duty, not just hunt buffalo," explained Pierre.

"I think we could fill out our number in Independence, there's quite a few trappers and others that don't come all the way to St. Louis and with the bottom dropping out of the beaver trade, there will probably be a few to be found there."

For the next hour, the men continued their discussion and planning while Emile and Clancy retired to the veranda to enjoy the morning sun and fresher air. "I know you spent most of your life living in the mountains, but I just can't imagine living with those heathen Indians. It just doesn't seem right somehow," commented Emile as she gathered her knitted shawl around her shoulders.

"I don't really see them as 'heathen' as you call them. Sure, they might not have a big church building with stained glass windows, but they have the majestic mountains and scenery that no artist with glass can duplicate. They, many of them, are just as 'religious' as most white men, but they have different names for the god they worship. And you'd be surprised at how many of them have placed their faith in our Lord Jesus Christ and worship the same God we do. My adopted father and mother, Jeremiah and Laughing Waters, actually led me to Christ. They taught me from the Bible, not just to improve my reading, but to know more about God. There are a lot of people with different colors of skin, that say they know the Lord, but they've never accepted Christ as their personal savior, have you?" she asked her friend and benefactor.

"Well of course, I've been going to church all my life!" declared Emile with surprise at the question.

"That's not what I asked. Has there been a time in your life that you personally accepted what Christ did on the cross for you? When he paid the price for your sins and mine so we could have the free gift of eternal life, he did that so we could receive his gift of salvation. And if you never asked Him to become your Savior and to receive that gift, all you are is religious and no different from those 'heathen' that don't know Christ," proclaimed Clancy with a tenderness in her voice and sincerity in her expression.

Emile looked at her young friend and furrowed her brow and asked, "Is that true? You mean I should ask God to forgive my sins and become my Savior? Is that what you mean by the gift of eternal life?"

"Yes, it is. That's God's simple plan of salvation."

"Hmmm . . . I'll have to think about that. Thank you for telling me that, I've never really understood it that way before." The older woman rocked her ladder back rocker with purpose and deep thought. Suddenly the screen door exploded open and the house-maid, Penny ran to the side of Emile and said, "Mrs. Em, Mrs. Em, come quick!" and spun on her heel to return to the house. "Now what on earth is the matter with that woman? Come with me, Clancy, let's go see what the problem is with that girl."

The two women rose to follow the panicked girl into the house. She led them to the bedroom of the patriarch, Pierre Sr., and turning to the two women explained, "He took sick right after he gots up from de table, Missy. He said he needed the bucket and fore I could gits it, he done upchucked all over de flo'!" She pointed to the old man that now sat on the floor and leaned against the interior wall, looked up at them with sadness filling his eyes and muttered, "I sure am sorry, Em. I just couldn't hold it. Could you get my son? I think I need him to help me to the privy." With a nod to Clancy, the older woman knelt beside the old man and tried to comfort him. Clancy walked quickly to the table where the two men were still discussing the preparations for the coming brigade.

"Mr. Chouteau, you need to come quickly, it's your father."

Without hesitation Pierre pushed himself up and spilling over the chair he hurried to the side of his father. After his father explained, Pierre helped him up and letting his father lean on his shoulder, the two men headed to the door and the outside privy. Upon their return, Pierre noted the mess had been cleaned up and the older man's bed was prepared for his return. Helping his father to the bed, he started to turn away when the older man motioned and asked for the chamber pot. It would be a long day at the Chouteau home.

As the two women spoke together in the kitchen, Emile and Clancy agreed that based on the symptoms as explained by Dr. McPheeters, their fear was Pierre Sr. was stricken with Cholera. Caleb stood on the veranda and awaited word about the patriarch and when Clancy joined him and shared her thoughts, he said, "Oh no, surely not." Clancy could only nod her head. While Clancy remained at the big house with Emile to offer any help, Caleb decided to start his work regarding the brigade and the journey back to the mountains. He returned to the cabin, exchanged his city attire for his buckskins, went to the stable for his mount and headed for the waterfront.

The ride through the streets of the city allowed Caleb to give thought to the many events of the past several days and the many plans contrived by the two partners in this new venture. Leaving his mount at the stable near the hotel, he checked his pistol in his waistband, dropped the length of his buckskin jacket over the handle and started his walk. As he passed the Hawken brothers storefront, he noticed another gunsmith just across the street. Pierre had told him about a new rifle that might be a good "buffalo gun" he decided to see what would be available. The sign over the door read 'Perkins and Hancock, gunsmiths' and a small bell rung as he pushed open the door. A bespectacled man with a bald head with just a half ring of hair that rested on his ears, looked up at the incoming visitor. Standing erect and setting down the tools he was using as he worked on a long gun on the counter, a broad shouldered middle-aged man that bore little fat on a muscular frame looked at the young man. A leather apron hung from his neck and showed considerable wear with oil stains and minute bits of metal and wood chips lying in the folds that were bunched around his waist. His voice did not match his size as a squeaky high pitch emanated from his whiskers and asked, "How can I help you?"

Caleb extended his hand as he said, "Good morning sir, I'm Caleb Thompsett. I'm looking to find that new-fangled rifle some folks are callin' a buffalo gun, do you know the one I mean?"

"You must mean the new Sharps. I just happen to have that rifle right over there," he stated as he motioned to the counter opposite where they stood. Making his way from behind his workbench/counter, he motioned for Caleb to follow him to the other side. He reached to the rack behind the counter, grasped a rifle that differed considerably from Caleb's familiar Hawken and held it before him. He explained, "This is a brand new rifle, I think I might have the first one from the maker and this is it. Now let me show you how it works, different from anything you've seen before." He began his instruction with an explanation of the falling block action, the double set triggers, which were like those on his Hawken, the hammer lock and the way the paper cartridges were used. He finished with, "And with these cartridges, you can get off eight to ten rounds per minute. Can you imagine?" he asked with pride. Then handing the rifle to Caleb, he watched as the young man fondled the weapon with admiration and obvious desire. The gunsmith added, "And with that much powder behind it, the maker swears it would be accurate up to five hundred yards!" Caleb looked at the man with disbelief and shook his head.

"I sure would like to try this on a buffalo, I bet I could put it to the test and see if it would really do the job at that distance."

"Buffalo? Have you really hunted buffalo?" asked the doubting gunsmith.

"Of course, I've dropped many of those big woolies with my Hawken, but not at any five hundred yards." Then laying the rifle on the counter, he looked at the nearby glass case and asked about a pistol that piqued his curiosity. The two men talked guns for the better part of an hour and before he left, Caleb had made a deal for the Sharps, several boxes of the paper cartridges, some that would have to be ordered in and would take a couple of weeks from New Orleans, a .44 Colt Dragoon revolver and a new .38 Colt Navy revolver for his wife. With a broad smile, a firm handshake, Caleb said, "I'll stop back by this afternoon to pick them up, but right now I need to get about my recruiting some men for the buffalo hunting brigade we're putting together. So if you run into any men that might be interested, be sure to tell them they can reach me through Pierre Chouteau." With a wave and a nod of his head, he left to make his way to the waterfront.

Going from tavern to tavern and stopping in any mercantile or any other business that looked like it might attract the type of men he was looking for, he accomplished little more than putting out the word he was looking for men. Occasionally he would see some men that expressed some interest, but none were quick to respond. As he walked down the riverfront, he thought of the stevedore that had offered his services to handle mules and Caleb decided to search the waterfront for the big man. As he passed each group of workers he would ask for 'a big man named Reuben' and receiving no answer, continued to the next group of workers laboring with bundles and crates at a large moored steamboat with towering stacks, three decks, and a gilded name plate stretching between the stacks that read, *Assiniboine*. This part of the levee had been paved with the cobblestones that stretched a short distance along the wharf. As he watched the workers he saw the familiar figure of the broad shouldered Reuben and Caleb lifted his hand to wave as he called out, "Hey there, Reuben!" The big black man, bare chested as usual, looked up at the approaching man, broke into a broad smile and said, "Yessuh boss, you da man wit da mule!"

"That's right! Say, do you have a couple minutes we might visit?" asked Caleb.

"Sho nuff, just lemme git this bundle over yonder an' I be right back."

When Reuben returned, he sat on a large crate next to Caleb and the young man began to explain the coming journey and asked if he would be interested in being a wrangler to about seventy-five mules and twenty horses. The big stevedore looked at Caleb with eyes wide with wonder and said, "You mean, ya'll are takin' that many mules and wagons out West to hunt buffalo? Whoooeeee, that's a lotta animals to tend to, yessuh. When do we leave?" he asked with a broad smile.

"Probably two to three weeks. If you want to come, you can either keep workin' here until we're ready to leave or you can help me find the animals and get the gear together. Your pay will start as soon as you come to work."

"Then boss, I's ready. I done had 'nuff o' dis' river and dis' place and I be glad to see the West wid you. Yessuh."

Morning was announced with a timid knock at the cabin door. Caleb rose from his seat at the table, leaving his tin coffee cup with its steaming liquid, and went to the door. Penny stood with bowed head and said, "Mr. Caleb, the missus done tol' me to tell you that Massuh Chouteau his own self done went to be wit' da Lawd," as she wiped tears from her cheeks and sniffled into her hanky.

Caleb answered, "Thank you Penny, we'll be coming to the big house shortly." As the house-maid trotted off to the main home, Caleb shut the door and looked at his wife standing behind him with bowed head. They held one another and allowed the memories to flood in, not just about Jean Pierre, but all loved ones lost. Whenever death visits, he brings with him the past with its 'what has been done' and pulls back the curtains of the future and all its 'what could have been'. As if the loss of a loved one does not bring sufficient grief, death adds the torment of random thoughts of torture to pound at the mind and hearts of those left stranded on the island of isolation. As if on cue, both released their grip and made ready for the visit to the grief stricken family.

At the request of Pierre and Emile, Clancy remained with the family to provide help and comfort especially for Emile, but Pierre and Caleb left to attend to the business and arrangements. Pierre visited with the undertaker while Caleb went to the warehouse to inform the workers and others. Caleb was surprised to see a small crowd of men lounging by the warehouse door and apparently waiting for the opening of the business. He noted that none had bundles of furs or other hides and then thought *Surely not all of these are here for the brigade!*

He entered the offices, shared the news of the death of the patriarch of the Chouteau family, then went to the warehouse to open the door to the waiting men.

As the door rolled back and let in the morning sun, the dregs of the waterfront crowded around the counter and clamored for answers to their many questions. Somewhat taken aback, Caleb raised his hands and said, "Hold on there, hold on. Step back a bit and let the rest of the men in here and I'll answer all your questions."

Then, turning back to the potbellied stove he poured himself a cup of steaming hot black coffee that was so black and thick it wouldn't have surprised the young man if it ate through the bottom of his cup. He turned and sat back on the counter, then lifted himself up to his full height to stand on the counter and looked over the upturned faces of the men below him. *Now that's quite an assortment of humanity, from the looks of them there's plenty of rascals and thieves as well as some experienced mountain men. Course there's some of 'em that ain't never seen a mountain or a buffalo.* With a big swallow of coffee, he sat his cup down and looked at the men and began.

"Now men, here's what we have planned . . ." and he went to considerable lengths to explain the trials and tribulations of the journey to include the many different Indian tribes that didn't want them coming. He explained about the buffalo, the country, the hard work of handling hides, driving mules and anything else he could think of that might discourage the weaker of the bunch including the need for everyone to do double duty. If they were hunters, they would share in the skinning and handling of hides. If muleskinners, they would share in loading and seeing to the animals and all men must be willing to help wherever needed without complaint. He concluded by saying, " . . . and if you sign up, you will be committing to stay with the brigade until we're done and come back with the hides. No quitting or running out, when a man gives his word, we expect him to honor it. If you're found drunk on the job, you'll lose your share of the take and we'll leave you where you are with nothing but a canteen of water and your rifle, if you have one. If you're a trouble maker, we'll set you alone in the wilderness and let the Indians have their way with you. Am I understood?" he asked as he looked over the bunch of restless men. "Are there any questions?"

"Yeah, who's gonna be the booshway fer this hyar

brigade?" asked the one known as Bear as he stifled a snicker.

"That'll be me, and what I say goes. When I tell you to do something, don't ask questions or hesitate because your life and the lives of the rest of the men may depend on it," replied Caleb as he stood spread legged with his fists on his hips and steel in his eyes.

Another called out, "How soon we be leavin'?"

"Just as soon as we have enough men and animals for the trek, it'll probably be in about a week, maybe two. Until then, we've made arrangements at the roomin' house just down the street for your bed and meals, and those of you that want to sleep under the trees, you can take your meals there. Once you sign on, we'll fetch you as we need you."

With no more questions, Caleb dropped to his customary place behind the counter and had the men line up to sign their names or make their mark. At the head of the line was the biggest mountain of a man Caleb had ever seen with thick black hair over his collar and a matching beard that obscured his neck, if he had one. He was outfitted in buckskins that appeared to have hung on his body for more than a year and had probably never been off in that time, judging by the smell of him. When Caleb lifted his eyes in askance for a name, he said, "I'm called Bear, that good 'nuff fer ye? And I been in the mountains before and kilt my share of buffler."

"Good, good. Sign your name or make your mark."

When Bear stepped aside, his shadow fell on a miniature version of the man. Standing no more than four feet tall, a grinning man with snaggle teeth and with a slight deformity that resembled dwarfism with a large chest, no neck, banty chicken legs but broad shoulders with muscular arms that now stretched to slick back his greasy blonde hair.

"They call me Catman," he snarled.

"Catman?" asked Caleb to be sure he heard the man right.

"That's right matey, Catman, cuz I got lots o' claws," he said in a voice just above a whisper as he spread wide his jacket and revealed a collection of knives hanging on the insides of the jacket and more in scabbards around his waist. "And they're all sharp as a razor."

"So are you signin' up as a hunter or skinner or just what is it you're thinking?"

"Why a skinner of course, but I can shoot my share as well."

And so it went for well over two hours, signing up the different men, turning some away that obviously would not be able to last the trip, and making notes about each one as to his impressions about their abilities and possibilities. He knew some would be problems, but he would thin out the bunch after he was done with his recruiting. Some would drop out of their own accord, but others would have to be sent packing. He could tell this was not going to be an easy task that was set before him, but he was anxious to get things started and this was just the first step of many.

There were some late arrivals and the intervals were filled as Caleb and Reuben discussed the locating of mules and horses. When Reuben told Caleb that he had little knowledge of the surrounding area, Caleb immediately thought of the young man at the first livery he boarded his horses with and instructed Reuben to see if he could get Brewster to come to the warehouse so Caleb could see if the young man could be of help to them. By late afternoon, Reuben returned with an excited Brewster skipping alongside the big black man. After Caleb explained what the brigade was doing and that they needed someone that knew their way around and could help Reuben and Caleb locate and buy mules and horses, the boy smiled broadly and said, "Why Cap'n, ain't nobody knows their way 'round better'n Brewster. I been all over this country at one time or 'nother. If I can't find whatchur lookin' fer, ain't nobody can, cep'n mebbe my friends Cracker and Pogo. Say Cap'n, could you use a couple more of us young'uns to take care o' things as we go out West?"

Caleb caught the expression of the boy and said, "As WE go out West? I didn't say you would go West with us, why you're just a boy, what could you do?" The boy struck a stance with feet spread wide, arms folded across his chest and his chin jutting out and answered, "Why, we can do anything any o' the rest o' ya kin do, cep'n we can do it faster!" he declared.

Both Reuben and Caleb snickered at the response and Caleb thought it would be handy to have some 'step'n'fetch its' around the camp. There would be plenty of tasks the men would shirk that would be just right for the youngsters. *Why, if the other two are anything like him, they'll probably be a bigger help than a lot of those that signed up. And they're good sized too and probably as old as some of these others when they struck out on their own. Yeah, I think they'll do.* "All right, you help out Reuben today and have your partners down here first thing in the morning. Now I won't tolerate shirkers, understand?"

"Yessir, Cap'n, I understand fine!"

Two matched, high-stepping Andalusian geldings with shiny coal black coats and flowing manes pulled the ornate funeral coach that boasted glass all around the highly polished carved ebony. Scalloped curtains accented the view of the maple casket that was highlighted with brass hardware. The slow moving coach was followed by a carriage drawn by a matched pair of dapple grey mares adorned with polished black harness that boasted silver conches. A top hat sat slightly askew on the grey bearded black man that handled the team with taut leads.

Seated in the carriage was Pierre and Emile Chouteau and Pierre's brother, François Chouteau. Other family members, children, nephews and nieces and others, walked behind the carriage. The procession traveled almost six blocks to St. Vincent de Paul cathedral where they were met by Father Jean Kiersereau who would conduct the service. The cathedral was packed with mourners and friends as Jean Pierre Chouteau and his family had been an important part of the city. It was Jean Pierre's father, René Auguste Chouteau that was the founder of St. Louis and the family had been an integral part of the entire community since its beginning.

After the service and internment, the family and many others returned to the estate. With an assortment of food, many just picked at the items on their hand held plates and mingled with those that offered condolences and prayers. After a couple hours of supporting their friends, the crowd dissipated and Caleb and Pierre left to attend to business at the warehouse. Caleb told Pierre about the many men that signed up, the arrangements made for their temporary lodging, the work undertaken by Reuben and the boys to begin the gathering of mules and horses, and concluded with, ". . . and we need to compile our supplies, get the wagons ready, finish with procuring the animals, and we can be underway," said Caleb with a smile of satisfaction. Pierre nodded his head in affirmation of the progress and looked aside with a pensive expression prompting Caleb to ask, "Are you sure you want to be doing this? Would you rather spend some more time at home with your wife? I can take care of these arrangements if . . . "

He was interrupted by Pierre, "No, no, I was just thinking how my father would be pleased with this project. He never would have thought about launching a Buffalo Brigade," he said with a chuckle. "What's next?"

"Well, if you want to make the arrangements for the different supplies, I thought I might take the men out and see what we've got. Maybe have some of them do a little shooting to see if they're worth anything. I think some of them would be better skinners than shooters, and some that think they can handle a mule might be more talk than anything. I'd rather know a little more about some of 'em before we commit to the trail," surmised Caleb.

"I think you're smart in that, and I'll leave it to you as to how many. I'm calculating on no more than a dozen wagons, ten or eleven for hides and the rest for supplies. It's up to you on how many shooters it'll take to fill that many."

"If they all had rifles like that new Sharps I picked up, it would be a lot easier. That thing can get off 8 to 10 shots in a minute, with that new paper cartridge, but I think I got the only one this side of the Mississippi. The gunsmith said the only reason he had one was because he had a brother who was also a gunsmith back East and helped him out. Same with that Colt Navy revolver, but I'll be glad to see if it lives up to expectations," commented Caleb.

Caleb sent two warehouse workers ahead to set up the prescribed targets while he made the arrangements for the freight wagons to pick up the men at the boarding house and those in the nearby woods. Early afternoon saw the three wagons unloading their unusual cargo of men that said they were shooters. After the shooters were aground, Reuben had the experienced teamsters put the prospective muleskinners through a short test to see if they could handle a four-up team. Two hundred yards downfield, the men had placed four posts with a brass gong suspended between each pair. As the men stood around, Caleb began to give the instruction. "This won't take long because we'll know right off if you hit the gong.

So, each man will take three shots. We want to see if you can hit the target and how quickly you can reload. Two men at a time and you can shoot from any position you like."

Bear and Catman stepped to the front, with Bear pushing others out of his way as he said, "Let me show you pilgrims how it's done." As he stood at an angle to the gong, his stance was replicated by the short Catman. Without any hesitation Bear pulled up, leaned slightly into his weapon, set the rear trigger, and squeezed off his first shot. A resounding clang from the gong and the swinging brass circle validated the hit. Catman let loose a hinged contraption from under the barrel of his rifle that dropped to the ground providing a support for the extended barrel. He quickly sighted, set his triggers, squeezed off the shot and his gong did a similar sounding and dance to verify his score. As they reloaded, both men dropped to one knee, squeezed off a hit, and went prone to repeat the score. As he stood to his full height, Bear roared a loud laugh and said, "And that's how it's done, boys. See if you can beat that!"

After all the shooters had their turn, Caleb loaded his Sharps and stepped to the line. He was anxious to see what the rifle could do. He lifted the rifle to his shoulder, looked at the rear peep sight and adjusted it for the distance, brought up the barrel to sight on the target and was starting to set the trigger when a burly voice from behind him said, "And what kinda rifle is it that you got there boy? I ain't never seen one o' them 'fore." The deep belly laugh told Caleb that the mocker was none other than Bear.

Caleb brought the rifle up again, set the trigger, took a breath and let it half way out, and slowly squeezed the front trigger. The roar that burst forth startled the shooters and each one jerked a little at the shock, but the sight of the distant brass gong being torn from it chains and sent spinning away hushed the crowd momentarily. A collective "Would you look at that!" let loose the flood-gates of chatter and questions. The accompanying noise distracted the shooters until within just seconds another roar shocked them into silence as another shot from the Sharps mimicked the previous one and the second gong broke its tether from one post and pulled the second post down as the gongs clanging sound was silenced when it struck the grassy ground below. After this second shot, the men just looked at their booshway and stepped back as he walked past.

All but two of the men that signed as shooters were able to score at least two out of three with the exception of two young men that were evidently from the city and their rifles were small bore squirrel guns and didn't have the range needed. Caleb drew the two aside and after finding out they were brothers and the only surviving members of their family, agreed to outfit them with new rifles and other gear. Their smiles and firm handshakes provided all the thanks that Caleb needed. The total number of shooters with the two brothers was fourteen, Caleb had thought twelve would be plenty but he also knew there would be some attrition, whether to disease, Indians or other causes, so he was pleased with his selection. Reuben had similar success with his muleskinners and by the end of the day, counting the skinners and other helpers, the Buffalo Brigade numbered forty-eight. Caleb and Clancy would round out the number to an even fifty. As Caleb thought about it, he shook his head and Reuben asked, "What is it boss, sumpin' the matta?"

"No, just thinkin' 'bout how many men we have and how I never thought I'd be charged with this kind of task." He also thought of the plans he made with James Heffernan about setting up a ranch in the Medicine Bow range and Heffernan's commitment to bring up a herd of cattle from Texas to start their ranch. His mind was full of what the future held. "But," he added as he looked up at his big friend, "with your help, we'll get it done!"

By the end of the week, Reuben and his helpers had procured forty-five mules and forty-six horses. They would need to buy more mules and horses en route to Independence from the many farms, but if unsuccessful they knew they could finish out the herd in Independence. Two freight wagons would accompany the brigade to Independence where ten more wagons would be added to their number. Pierre had purchased the necessary supplies, food, powder and lead, additional clothing items, bedrolls and trade goods that would be necessary for the first leg of the trip. Additional supplies would be waiting in Independence, dropped off by Captain LaBarge at the Chouteau warehouse. Departure would be on the morrow, the first of July, 1849.

THE SUN STRUGGLED TO DAUB THE TREETOPS WITH the gold of the morning as Caleb and Clancy finished packing the panniers for their pack mule. Without the need for daily provisions, which would be on the freight wagons for the Buffalo Brigade, there was ample room for their personal items of clothing and gear, though they chose to leave behind the paraphernalia of the city. Caleb slipped his Sharps in the saddle scabbard and Clancy did likewise with her Hawken. Caleb's Hawken, Clancy's bow and quiver of arrows, the extra paper cartridges for the Sharps and other necessities were also secured to the pack saddle on the mule.

Caleb had withdrawn the bulk of their wealth from the bank in the form of gold coin which was now secured in the false bottomed parfleches and saddle bags. Once again, the pouches of molded gold and lead covered musket balls were hidden in plain sight in the pouches that hung from the saddle horns to the front of the pommels of the saddles. They led their horses and mule to the hitch rail at the front of the big house, mounted the veranda and met Emile and Pierre as they exited the doorway to greet the young couple.

The rising sun cast blinding white-gold rays that painted long shadows the length of the veranda as Emile embraced Clancy with her motherly tiptoe hug while Pierre and Caleb clasped hands then pulled one another to a hug and pats on the back.

"Well my friend, you're off on another great adventure and I can't say I'm not envious," stated Pierre as he held the hand of Caleb and patted his shoulder while looking into his eyes. It was an embarrassed but confident expression that covered the face of the man that stood before the elder statesman and now patriarch of the Chouteau family.

"You have been a good friend and I think of you as another father. Clancy and I will never forget all you've done for us," shared Caleb. "Without your help, I'm afraid we would have been just another pair of drifters that was swallowed by this monstrous city. Thank you, my friend."

Emile interjected, "But you two have been a great blessing to us and we are so thankful to have you with us these past months. Please come back and stay again," she pleaded as she looked to the tall redhead. Clancy smiled and bent to give her friend another strong embrace.

"We've got people waiting for us, so we better get a move on," said Caleb as he touched Clancy's elbow. She nodded, dabbed at a tear and turned to join her husband as they walked down the steps and mounted their horses. With a wave and a nod, they kneed their horses to begin their journey. Emile turned to her husband and said,

"They make such a handsome couple, especially when they're in their buckskins, they are the picture of the wild West." Pierre answered his wife with a simple, "Ummhummm," as they made their way back into their home.

In the past few days before the scheduled departure, Caleb had watched the many men as they worked around the corrals and warehouse preparing for the journey. Often visiting with them, assigning tasks, and working alongside, he was judging the character of the men to select certain ones to lead the brigade. He also noted that true to his instinct, Bear and Catman would be a challenge to handle and he was also concerned that some of the others were beginning to hang around the pair and follow their example. But Caleb had noted others that had impressed him with their work and manner and the young man had selected some to help in the leading of the brigade. As his lieutenant he chose an equal to Bear, a man known as Red Pierce. Red was similar in size and strength as Bear, but had long reddish blonde hair and a beard that reached to the middle of his massive chest. To say he resembled a barrel would be an understatement as his shoulders were broad and his chest deep and he tapered to railroad tie sized legs that supported his almost three hundred pounds. Yet for all his size, his manner was non-confrontational but he seemed to be holding an internal monster in check as he busied himself with work.

To lead the muleskinners Caleb chose an older man that was of good size but kindly features that reminded Caleb of his mother's stories of Kris Kringle. Don Brown had been the ram-rod of a freighter company before he lost his family to the Cholera epidemic and he now wanted to escape the memories. A man with considerable experience behind him, Jesse Sparger was chosen to oversee the rest of the men that were not shooters. The animals would be the responsibility of Reuben and his boys. Jody Clark would be the cook with Reuben's friend, Lazarus as his helper.

As the couple approached the gathered men, he allowed a slight grin to pull at one corner of his mouth as he watched them take in the sight of a woman and nudge one another, often talking behind their uplifted hands. He knew Clancy was an impressive beauty and he thought she was especially stunning in her buckskin outfit. With knee high fringed moccasins with her leggings tucked in the tops, her long tunic draped past her hips and showing the bright designs of beads and quills on the yoke and her red hair cascading past her shoulders, she caught the attention of every man. But her stoic expression showed nothing but confidence and determination. Draped from her belt was a custom made holster that carried her new Navy Colt revolver at an angle by her left hip. It would be an easy grab with her right hand and rested lazily at her waist. The revolver was like a warning sign to anyone that let his gaze linger too long.

Handing the reins of his mount and the lead rope of the mule to his wife, Caleb dropped to the ground and mounted the seat of the nearest freight wagon raising his hands for the attention of the men. "All right men," he began, "this buffalo brigade is the first brigade of its kind. As you know, we're not going after beaver or any other varmint that we have to wade in the water for, but like I told you when you signed up, you will abide by what we said or we'll set you out on your own. Now those of you that have never been West and been among the Indians, you especially have to do as you're told because not only your life but the lives of every one of these men might depend on it.

Most of you know who the other men are that're leadin' with me, but let me set you straight about sumpin'! If any of these men tell you to do sumpin' you do it without question or face the penalty. We don't have time for baby-sittin' or molly-coddlin' anyone, so from here on out you're expected to pull your own weight. Understand me?" he asked as he surveyed the upturned faces of the men. He continued, "Now my wife and I will do the scoutin' and most of the huntin' and we'll be out front ahead of the rest of ya'. Red there, " he motioned to the big man astride a tall black gelding, "is my right hand man and he'll be in charge in my absence," as he spoke he noted the response and grumbling coming from Bear and those around him, "and what he says goes!"

Caleb looked down at Don Brown sitting on the wagon seat where he stood and asked, "Are you ready to head out?"

"I'm as ready as an old maid waitin' fer her first kiss!" replied the boss of the muleskinners. He would drive the first wagon and his chosen second would follow in the other. Red had the many men lined out with some following the wagons ahead of the mules and spare horses, while a larger number would follow the herd. All the men, shooters, skinners and helpers alike would double as herders on the first leg of the trip. Caleb dropped to the ground, motioned to the men to mount up as he joined Clancy, and shouted to Brown, "Move 'em out!"

Red Pierce, impressive in his fringed buckskins and cradling his Hawken in a beaded and fringed white tanned buckskin sheath, lifted his rifle to signal the men to follow after the wagons.

Caleb and Clancy gigged their horses to the front of the entourage and pointed the way on the road that led to the distant trees on the shore of the Missouri River. They would follow the South bank of the Missouri on a well-traveled road that would take them to Independence, the jumping off place of many West bound wagon trains. And the journey of the Buffalo Brigade was underway.

STANDING TALL IN HIS STIRRUPS, LIFTING HIS HEAD high, Caleb sucked in lungs full of the woodsy air. Turning to Clancy he said, "Well, it ain't as cool and clear as the mountains, but it sure beats what we were breathing in the city! Don'tcha think?"

"Yeah, at least it don't smell like sewage and death. But this country sure gets muggy and hot, I'm 'bout ready to ride out into the middle of that river just to cool off a mite," answered Clancy as she pointed with her chin to the muddy Missouri that slowly moved along pushing the debris from a recent rain. They were following a good roadway that locals called *Boon's Lick Trail* because it was used by salt wagons bringing much needed salt to the city. The main roadway to the West, this trail joined the Santa Fe Trail at Boonville and the buffalo brigade would take that roadway to Independence. The two rode side-by-side with the mule keeping pace with his plodding and mindless gait as he followed. With eyes continually roving to watch for any danger but not expecting any, Caleb enjoyed the 'review' of his wilderness education received on his first trip from the East. He looked at the towering Elm and Oak that were interspersed with an occasional cluster of Black Walnut and remembered Scratch telling him how to identify the different trees by their size, bark and leaves. Closer to the riverbank he noted a couple of Dogwood and a random Redbud. To his left the woods were so thick with close growing trees and underbrush, it appeared as a broad green curtain. Closer to the roadway a wide variety of flowers and grasses kept Caleb guessing as to their names and uses.

The gentle rocking gait of the long-legged appaloosas had both riders sitting comfortable when suddenly both horses spooked and crow-hopped to avoid a bristle backed long-tusked grunting hog that warned them to beware as she led her litter of pigs across the roadway into the thick cover of the woods. Both riders kept their seats and with firm pulls on the reins to lift the heads of their mounts, they struggled to keep control as they watched the hog family disappear. Reining up the horses, they spoke softly to them as they leaned over and patted their necks to reassure them and calm the animals down. While all the commotion was going on the pack mule didn't miss a step and calmly looked at the horses and riders with an expression of disbelief.

"That's the first time I ever saw one o' them! I heard 'bout 'em, but ain't never seen one, till now," declared Caleb.

"Really? I've seen 'em before, but that was when I was little and we were on our way out West. My Mum said they were purty good eatin' but I wouldn't want to leave the little'ns without their momma."

"Ahh, we'll get somethin' soon 'nuff. I think these woods oughta be full of game," observed Caleb in answer. Through the remainder of the day the couple spotted many different animals, squirrels, chipmunks, coyote, fox and a few other rodents like weasel and raccoon, but it wasn't until later afternoon they finally bagged a white tail buck that would be enough meat for one meal with their crew. Hanging the carcass by the trail, they continued on to find a spot for their first night's camp and within a couple of miles a sizable clearing opened beside the road and was quickly chosen by the pair for the camp. The grassy clearing was about five acres in size and would provide ample graze for the animals and the edge of the woods would give shelter for the men. Caleb and Clancy began to set up their camp that would be off from the main cook fires of the brigade but near enough for Caleb to set up watches and give the needed directions for the camp. With this being their first night on the trail, he knew a pattern would need to be established for the order of the camp and the men's routine responsibilities.

Everyone pitched in to make a good camp. The animals were controlled with a combination of the wagons forming a portion of the perimeter, the camp at the edge of the trees and a series of rope and brush barricades. It would take some time before everything became routine, but the control of the animals seemed to be well in hand with the direction of Reuben. Some of the men complained about a black man giving orders, but when their complaints fell on deaf ears they soon abandoned their griping. The cook was quick with his work, with deer steaks skewered over the fire and dripping juices into the flames and several large pots of beans hanging over the second cook fire. Four large Dutch ovens with biscuits sat on pile of hot coals that matched those resting on the rimmed lids. Men were busy with bedrolls and tack around the perimeter with each finding what he thought would be the softest bed of leaves. Although their camp was separate, Caleb and Clancy chose to join the men for the first night's meal and casually strolled to find a seat on one of the large logs near the fire.

The last light of the day was fighting with the crowding darkness before the cook shouted, "Come and Get it! Grab yore plates, pick a steak, an' I'll give ya' some beans and biscuits! First man that complains gets to go to the end of the second line!"

One of the first men in line looked over his shoulder and said to the cook, "Why Cookie, there's only one line!"

"If you complain, you'll be at the end of the next line which won't form up till breakfast, ya' unnerstand?" The other men chuckled and told the first, "Go 'head and gripe about it pilgrim, I'll take your place in line!" With a little pushing and shoving, a lot of banter and laughter, the crew made their way through the line and filled their plates. Seating themselves around the main campfire, idle conversation filled the evening air as men laid the foundations of friendship and camaraderie. Trust would be long in coming as these men had come from different walks of life, standards of living, and a variety of moral upbringing. Many had experienced great loss in the fire and epidemic while some had never claimed either family or home, others never knew true kinship with any other living thing. With backgrounds a diverse as slavery and wealth, the amalgam of humanity paralleled that of the West they were bound for and with broad strokes painted a picture of an infant nation.

Looking around the gathering of men, Caleb watched and listened and the stolen glances at his wife did not go unnoticed. Most of the company casually lounged and carried on conversations spawned from curiosity, but there were others that spoke in muted tones and shielded their words with carefully placed hands or turned heads. Low rumbles of complaining and fault-finding came from the small group near the outspoken Bear and his cunning companion. *I'm gonna have trouble with that bunch, sure as shootin'* thought Caleb, then turning to the nearby Red Pierce he nodded to the group of conspirators and an answering nod from the red bearded giant indicated his awareness of the budding problem.

Clancy made it a point not to look directly at any of the men but she was civil to all, remaining close by her husband's side. Her long hair tumbled in curls over her collar and none were aware of her between the shoulders scabbard that carried her razor sharp Bowie knife. She felt confident in her own abilities with both the Navy Colt and the Arkansas toothpick and did not give way to any of the men and their leering stares. But Caleb noted those that were more brazen than others and knew there would have to be a time they were put in their place. Nothing was more important than the safety of his wife and he would bear no disrespect of his mate, yet he was also aware of Clancy's abilities and that any lessons given would be best learned if she was one of the teachers. *There'll be plenty of opportunities to make our point without rushing things, we'll just wait and see,* thought the young leader of the brigade.

The rest of the week quickly became routine with twenty or more miles made every day. Passing through towns and villages like Miller's Landing, a long established trading post, and Loose Creek, a small settlement at the junction of the Osage River and the Missouri, that held nothing but a combination mercantile and post office, there was little else to break the monotony of the thickly wooded roadsides and the slow moving river. Travel was easy with the wide and well used roadway. Game was plentiful and men worked better with full stomachs. Friendships were forming and as encouraged, the men began to partner up with the common sight of groups of two and three riding together and pitching bedrolls near one another. With partners, it was easier to keep track of the many travelers so stragglers would not be left behind or those with difficulties would not be missed. The men had become comfortable with the chosen leaders and responded well to the directions given.

Nearing the half way point, Caleb informed the men they would be camping outside of Boonville and they would have an opportunity to visit the town for the night, but they had to give everyone time to visit by taking turns at minding the camp. Straws were drawn and times allotted for each one to make their visit to the town and have time for a meal and a drink or two, but all were cautioned about drunkenness and brawling. Caleb reminded them that "You cause any trouble or drink too much, you could be left behind and would forfeit any pay you have comin' to ya."

With a shout and a holler, the first group mounted up and gigged their horses toward the town of Boonville. Caleb stayed behind with Clancy and others and said, "I sure hope no trouble comes from this." The answering nod from his wife shared his concern. Caleb had sent a man ahead to give ample warning to the settlement that had been named after the sons of the famed frontiersman, Daniel Boone. A sizable community, the town was nestled at the junction of the Missouri River and the Lamine River and was the beginning of the Santa Fe Trail that was the well-established route for trade to the Southwest and Mexico. It was here that the buffalo Brigade would leave the Missouri River and follow the smaller Blackwater River and the Santa Fe Trail into Independence. With this being the half-way point between St. Louis and Independence, Caleb felt the men needed a change and begrudgingly allowed the trip to town. He just hoped he wouldn't regret it.

THE LAST HALF OF THE BIG MOON HUNG SUSPENDED in the midst of the black velvet sky. The diamond tipped stars were playing a game of hide and seek behind the few remaining clouds that lingered past their bedtime. Clancy was sleeping soundly in her bedroll with the pup cuddling close, near the smoldering campfire while Caleb leaned back against the big log and listened to the noise from the larger cook fire and the camp of the men. The first group had returned with a few happy drunks, but none beyond self-control, but Caleb was more concerned with the second group. Bear, Catman and their followers had purposefully chosen the second group knowing they would have the later hours of the night for their drinking and carousing.

He looked heavenward and noting the few remaining stars reckoned the coming of the morrow would soon be at hand. Just then the clatter of hooves of returning horses mixed with the raucous shouts and singing marked the return of the second group. Caleb stood and started for the cook fire to see if all the men returned. He was greeted by the one that always made him think of a snake with his squinting eyes and grin that showed just two teeth that resembled the fangs of a snake, Rupert Michaels said, "Howdy Cap'n! Yore just like my Ma used to be, waitin' up fer us wayward chillun'. But we made it Cap'n! Well cep'n fer Bear and Cat," as he let loose a belly laugh that was interrupted by a long belch, "the local constab, uh constab . . ., uh sheriff, he he, decided to put 'em up fer the night."

"That's right, boss. After they kinda broke up the place, specially that big picture o' that woman oer' the bar that Bear said looked like his dear ol' Mother. Anywhoo, the Sheriff said he'd be sleepin' it off in his hoosegow till he weren't drunk no more an' he paid fer his wreckin' the place!" stated another member of the follow along group known as John-John The rest of the group staggered to their bedrolls with most just crashing down and snoring before their heads hit the saddles.

Caleb walked among the bedrolls counting heads to see if the two troublemakers were the only ones missing. He made a second round and count just to be sure and found a couple under the wagon that he missed the first time around. Satisfied that all were present, he returned to his bedroll beside Clancy and sought the elusive sleep that would soon be chased away with the coming dawn.

Red stood over the slumbering form of Caleb and nudged his foot to wake the young man. Rolling over and rising to his elbows, he looked up at the bushy red beard that obscured the view of Red's face, but the mellow voice brought him full awake. "What are we goin' to do 'bout them two troublemakers?" he drawled.

Sitting up and rubbing his face and eyes to dispel the sleepiness, Caleb asked the big man, "What do you think we ought to do?"

"That's your call, but we did say if they were caught drunk on the job, we'd leave 'em. Course they weren't on the job and just in town, but that's a fine line, I figger."

As Caleb stretched to his full height, arched his back to remove the kinks, he said, "I think better after I've had me some coffee." He motioned to Red to follow him to the big cook fire and the swinging coffee pot. Other men were slowly coming back to reality after their night in the town and escape from the trail, as the two leaders filled their tin cups with the black brew. Seating themselves on a log just back from the fire, they downed a good swig of the bitter tasting blackness and shaking their heads in unison, Caleb said, "Whoooeeee, what did Cooky make this with? What is it, his sure cure for hangovers?" Red answered with a choking swallow followed by a nod of his head that reverberated in the long whiskers over his chest.

"I'm thinkin' we need to go to town and get those two outta there so we don't ruin the reputation of the company, and we can figger out what to do with 'em when we get back. I don't want the rest of the men thinkin' we didn't mean what we said, but neither do I want 'em thinkin' we can't be fair with 'em," surmised the young leader.

"Good 'nuff. I'll get the horses," replied Red then

turned back to Caleb, "Are we gonna rest up here, or do you want ta' get started soon's we get back?"

"I'm not sure, let the men rest till we get back then we'll decide."

As they approached the town, Caleb noted the outlying Salt Licks with several men shoveling the salt into the nearby wagons. Caleb had intentionally bypassed the larger city of Jefferson City, the capital of Missouri, to avoid this type of problem, believing the men could be better controlled within the confines of the smaller community. Now his theory was being put to the test.

It was a sizeable and busy community that greeted the two buck skinners. The long main street showed a variety of businesses, saloons, and cross roads that led to the back streets with their clapboard homes. They passed the usual outlying livery stable with a corral that held several horses and mules. Caleb nodded to the corral and said to Red, "Maybe we oughta check with the livery man and see if we can get any of those mules. Reuben said we needed about two dozen more."

"Yup, probly' oughter check with him before we go to the jail," suggested Red. Caleb reined his horse to the livery and both men dismounted in front of the big double barn doors as a sizeable man with a leather apron, obviously the blacksmith, greeted the pair. "What can I do fer you gents? Needin' to put your horses up?"

"Howdy," greeted Caleb, then continued, "No, but we are interested in those mules you got in the corral there, any of 'em for sale?"

"Why shore 'nuff. I got six or seven back there we might make a deal on, iffn' yore interested."

After the dickering and examining, the men settled on six of the seven mules and the livery man agreed to keep them and the horses until the men returned. Caleb took to the boardwalk and three doors down they entered the sheriff's office and jail. As they entered the sheriff looked them over and said, "I hope you're here for that big boy back yonder," he said with a wave over his shoulder in the direction of the cells beyond the barred door.

"If your big boy is the same as ours, then yes we're here to at least talk about it. What's it gonna take to spring him?" asked Caleb.

"Well, normally, it'd cost you ten dollars plus the damages, but if you'll just pay the damages I'd be happy as a fat frog to let you have him," croaked the potbellied sheriff.

"How'd you get him in here anyway," asked Red, "he's a purty big fella and you ain't all that big. What'd you have to do?"

The mostly bald man that was showing his age dropped his feet from his desk, pulled a drawer out and withdrew a belaying pin, "This is my equalizer! A little souvenir from me sailing days, matey!" He held up the pin, slapped it to his palm, then with another swing he slammed it to his desk, denting the wood near other similar dents, and added, "This makes it real easy to put a prisoner to sleep for a good long nap. Course with that'n back yonder, it took four men to carry him here from the saloon, but he woke up a bit ago, and I'm anxious to get rid of him. It's bad 'nuff that he's so blamed loud, that wouldn't be so bad, but he stinks! Even the other drunks that've been sleepin' in their own vomit are complainin' cuz he smells so bad! Yessir, you git him outta here and I won't charge you a thing."

Caleb laughed then asked, "How much you willin' to pay us to take him?" grinning wide.

"Hah! Don't tempt me, if you don't take him, I might just resign to get away from that odoriferous hulk. I'd call him a skunk but that would be an insult to all them striped kitties out there."

Still chuckling, Caleb and Red led the way for the two troublemakers to follow to the livery. Bear and Catman had lodged their mounts there before their drunken spree and now gladly mounted up to get out of town. With the mules on stringers, the troublesome duo each were given the task of leading three each as Caleb and Red led the way back to camp. The two drunks were suffering with the effects of a bad hangover from cheap rotgut whiskey and whatever else they consumed from the night before and when Cooky offered some left over scraps for their breakfast, they declined in favor of a tin cup of stiff coffee.

Clancy was seated on a log and was visiting with the two brothers that were the last two to sign up for the trip. Both cotton-tops, Clancy thought they were not much older than sixteen but she didn't ask, Chance and Colton Threet were enamored with the red headed woman. They shared a moment that brought some light laughter as Bear and Catman seated themselves opposite the fire on another large log and holding their coffee with trembling hands. The laughter from the three prompted a response from Bear as he grunted, "What're you laughin' at? You two pups ain't big 'nuff to lick my boots, now hush up!" then looking at Clancy he added, "And why don't you, little missy, come on over here an' let me show you what a real man is like?"

Caleb and Red were approaching the coffee pot when Caleb heard the talk and turned to hear the big man make his crude remark. He looked to his wife and caught her eye and a slight nod of her head and he knew not to interfere. Clancy looked at the big man and replied, "So, just what do you think a real man is cuz everyone around here sure knows you ain't one!"

He spit out his coffee and roared, "Git over here an' I'll show you zactly what a real man is cuz you ain't never had one like me!" Clancy had moved her hand to her shoulder as if to flip her hair back, but with a sudden move she grasped the handle of the Bowie, flipped it forward and buried it, sharp edge up, just below the big man's crotch. He yelped with a scream that startled everyone as he looked down at the sharp edge of the knife that just opened a small slit in his buckskins to reveal his red longhandles. As he froze and stared at the knife, he jerked his head up to curse the woman but was instantly silenced as he stared at the black hole of death at the end of the barrel of Clancy's Navy Colt held just inches from his forehead.

"Wha . . ." he muttered as he sucked air and froze in fear. As he started to move she cocked the hammer and said, "Don't do it," with a calm but firm voice that was heard by everyone nearby. Catman started to open his jacket but as he stretched his hand to grab a knife, the sound of another cocking hammer stopped him. Slowly turning his head, he saw another one-eyed barrel staring him down. It was the heavy Colt Dragoon held in the steady hand of Caleb that nailed him to the log. Clancy looked at her husband out of the corner of her eye and smiled with her mischievous grin and spoke to the big man, "Now shuck 'em!"

Nervously, the bear of a man asked, "Whatchu mean, shuck 'em?"

"Your buckskins, shuck 'em!"

"I ain't gonna take off my clothes, are you crazy?" whined the big man.

"You take 'em off, or I'll cut 'em off!" she ordered, as she displayed another Bowie handed to her by her husband. Slowly the big man stood, and as the rest of the men gathered around, he dropped his beaded belt with its knife and scabbard, then he drew the tunic over his head. Looking askance at his captor, she nodded her head and motioned with the cocked pistol, and said, "Them too."

He bent to remove his knee high moccasins, then lowered his breeches revealing his ragged faded red union suit with the rear flap hanging by one button. Clancy ordered, "Now move," as she motioned to the backwater eddy of the river. He walked before her holding the flap with one hand and the other raised over his head, with all the men following and Catman beside him and looking back at the Colt in Caleb's hand. As they crossed the small sandbar, Caleb told Catman to strip and join Bear in the water. Cooky had grabbed a couple bars of lye soap and tossed them to the two bathers with a

"Here ya go, scrub all that stink off, we're tired of your smell ruinin' our meals!"

The rest of the men jeered and laughed and echoed the sentiments of the cook. The two troublemakers begrudgingly started scrubbing until Bear said, "This ain't right! I ain'ta gonna do it!" But when his reluctance was met by a shot from Clancy that split the floating bar of soap, he quickly grabbed the pieces and scrubbed with both hands. One of the men had grabbed their buckskins and threw them after the duo and hollered, "Scrub these too, they stink as bad as you do!" to another round of laughter from the crew.

While the two humbled but now sober objects of ridicule finished their scrubbing, the rest of the men prepared to resume their journey. The Santa Fe trail split off from the Boone Lick Trail, just south of the city and the brigade took the new roadway before noon. This day would not yield the usual twenty miles, but Caleb thought the harvest of humbled workers would be much more profitable. At least, he hoped it would.

THE SECOND DAY OUT OF BOONVILLE BROUGHT THE brigade to the confluence of the Blackwater and Davis Rivers. Having crossed five rivers already, the brigade had gained confidence with their experience and started this crossing without any undue delay. The riverbanks were crowded with an abundance of bank hugging trees and shrubs but the crossing was wide with good footing.

With the wagons leading out, Reuben and the men pushed the mules and horses into the water without difficulty. As the animals approached the mid-way point, the bottom dropped away and they visibly dropped into the deeper water, and without the familiar footing, many of the animals grew wide-eyed then started swimming gaining confidence with each stroke of their long legs. With heads high, nostrils flaring, the crowded animals grunted with every stroke and the deep water took little time to cross.

Pushing sixty animals across were twenty men following the herd and about ten men on each side. On the upstream side, a shout rang out that got the attention of nearby riders but could not be heard by the others with the noise of the animals and water. Jesse Sparger saw a twisted log with outstretched branches moving with the current towards the herd, but the branches were moving. As he moved closer, he watched helplessly and out of reach as the log collided with one of the riders, the Mexican, Juan Alvarez. He screamed as the branches, now recognized as a knot of several water moccasins, engulfed the rider and muffled his screams as he fought and flailed but was drug from his horse into the current. The log and the commotion with the panicked horse startled the herd and pandemonium broke loose with some animals trying to turn around and return to the bank and others climbing atop those obstructing their escape. With the screaming of animals, braying of mules and yelling of nearby riders, every man spurred his horse to escape to the bank. Jesse nudged his animal to the last spot he saw Juan, but the only evidence was the muddy water and a floating serape. He grabbed it, looked downstream for any sign of life, and made his way to the far bank. Horses and mules were dragging themselves from the melee and men were trying to regain control. A short way inland, Reuben and the boys had circled the herd into a slow moving mob that were shaking themselves free of water and searching for graze.

Red rallied all the men, checked to see if anyone was missing besides Juan and asked Jesse to say a word of prayer for the man so they could get on with the day's ride. Jesse asked his God to deliver Juan if he still lived, but if not to welcome him home and asked for God's hand to protect the rest of them on the remainder of the journey. The men replaced their head coverings and silently moved get the herd back on the trail.

The Santa Fe trail that started in Boonville, began as a winding trail big enough for narrow wagons but with the continued and increased travel by the many pilgrims going West to Oregon and the movement of the Mormons going to the promised land, it had become a wide roadway that made travel easy for both the freight wagons and the herd of the buffalo brigade. Twenty miles a day was common and thirty miles was not unusual. Four more days brought the travelers over the last rise outside of Independence. "There it is! That's Independence," proclaimed Caleb to his wife as he stood in his stirrups and stretched his arm to point. Clancy looked at him and asked, "How do you know that's Independence? It could be some other town, I thought we wouldn't get there for another day or two."

"I can tell because of the river. See there, that's the Missouri that makes that big bend just north of town, don't you remember when we came through here on the St. Ange?" As she stroked the head and shoulders of the pup that stood with feet on either side of the saddle horn and his chin resting on the horn, she looked at her husband and giggled at his excitement. Clancy smiled broadly and said, "You're just like a little kid, you're so excited."

Sitting back in his saddle and looking at his wife he said, "Truth is, I was wonderin' if we would even make it this far. With all the things that have happened, and knowing we have so far to go I was wonderin' if I didn't bite off more'n I could chew! But we made it, and after we get outta this country and back where we can see farther than the next tree, I'll feel better about it all."

The pushing of the herd of mules and horses through the broad street caused the business men and spectators alike to line the boardwalk and crane their necks to visually examine this unusual phenomenon. The trail weary mules moved like docile animals but that appearance was deceiving, these mules had proven themselves to be trail wise and herd smart. Most of the herders had come to respect the intelligence of these lop eared animals and realized that where a horse might push through any obstacle, the mule would stop and examine it and determine the best way around it and then proceed. Their deliberation was often mistaken for stubbornness. It was that realization that prompted Red to trade his long legged black gelding for a jack mule of equal size but greater smarts. Red now pushed the herd toward the open gate of the large corral behind the Chouteau warehouse that bore the American Fur Company name emblazoned across the front. Seeing everything was well in hand, Caleb and Clancy tethered their animals at the front hitch rack and stepped to the boardwalk and into the main door of the warehouse. As he walked to the counter, a large buckskin clad bearded man, obviously a trapper, bumped shoulders with Caleb, muttered his excuses and went to the door.

As Caleb watched the big man leave, he turned and asked the counter clerk, "Who was that man?"

"Why, that's Jim Beckwourth, he's purty well known up in the mountains. He married a Crow squaw and they made him one of their chiefs, then he went to Californie, and he just brought in a load of furs. He's partnered up with us afore," stated the clerk. "What can I do fer you? You got some furs or sumpin'?"

"You're supposed to have some wagons and supplies for us, I'm Caleb Thompsett."

"Oh yessir, I was lookin' fer a much older man, but we got those wagons for you all right. They're right out back, ten of 'em, they're lined up against the back fence and all the harness and stuff you need is in the beds of the wagons. Mr. Chouteau arranged for the supplies to be stacked in the back of the warehouse so it'll be easier to get 'em loaded in the wagons. Oh, and a Mr. Heffernan was in here this morning asking for you. Said he'd be at the Savoy hotel and he'd like to talk to you before you leave." With a nod of the head, Caleb took Clancy's elbow while her arm cradled the pup, and steered her to the door. They put their horses and mule in the corral with the other animals, their tack on the top rail of the fence, and gathered the men together.

"Men, we'll be headin' out early in the mornin' and until then you're on your own," and receiving a loud cheer from the men, he lifted his hands and continued. "Now listen and listen good. Any man that gets into trouble will be on his own, we're not bailin' anybody outta jail or payin' any damages, and if you show up drunk in the mornin' and can't do your job, you will be left behind, is that clear?" The men gave a scattering of positive answers, but Caleb noticed the reaction of Bear and Catman and a few of their followers. But he continued, "I've arranged it that you can put your bedrolls down in the warehouse or stable here and you leave the horses here. I've got a twenty-dollar gold piece for each of you as wages so far, so you're on your own for your eats and drinks. Now, enjoy yourselves but stay outta trouble!" With that he stepped down from the wagon bed, and helped Clancy pass out the gold pieces provided by the company.

The Savoy hotel was typical of the time with a restaurant on the main floor and rooms on the second and third floor. Clancy was pleased when she discovered a hot bath would be available and she quickly decided to enjoy the luxury. Caleb also partook of the pleasure and by early evening the two, leaving the pup to snooze alone in the room, were now attired in their clean set of buckskins, the same set they were married in, walked into the restaurant and caught the eye of every diner. Caleb knew they looked at him as an afterthought as the beauty of the white tanned buckskin highlighted by an abundance of blue and white beads with quills and elk ivory simply accented the red headed lovely they adorned. Only moments after they were seated, James Heffernan arrived at their table and asked to join them. Caleb was relieved when all James' attention was focused on their conversation and did not give undue attention to Clancy.

After dinner was over and the casual conversation ebbed James scooted closer to the table, put both elbows before him and looked intently at Caleb, then began, "Caleb, I know we talked a lot about the possibility of a ranch in the mountains but we never definitely settled anything. All the way here while I was on the riverboat, I thought about it. The more I've thought about it the more determined I am to see it come to fruition. Now, here's what I propose. If you go to the place in the mountains you spoke about, build your home and do your best to prepare for cattle, you know, some corrals, a barn and whatever else you can do, then I will bring up a herd of about a thousand head to get things started. I'm going to Texas, leaving in the morning, with a supply mule train that's taking the Santa Fe trail to Taos. From there I can hire some hands and go to Texas where my brother in law and sister have the cattle we need. We'll bring the herd up next spring. Now how does that sound?"

"Well, James, we've been giving it a lot of thought too and we're kinda gettin' used to the idea. Now mind you, we're not ranchers, actually I ain't never even seen many cattle, much less know what to do with 'em, but the idea sounds pretty good. I figger we can learn what we don't know and make a go of it.

We're plannin' on buildin' us a home in the Medicine Bow basin or at least in the foothills at the edge of the basin, and I figger that'll make pretty good ranch country. There's quite a few wild horses round about there, and I might be able to get a couple hands to join us. But, there's one thing I want clear, if you don't like that country or don't think you can make a go of it or whatever, I stand ready to just buy those cows and do it on my own. Now if you're willing to commit to that, that I can buy you out and likewise you can buy me out, then let's do it!" declared Caleb as he looked from James to Clancy and let a broad smile stretch his face.

James reached across the table and offered his hand to shake Caleb's and seal the deal. The two men shook hands vigorously and James said, "Let's have a drink on that!"

"Well now, I never did develop a taste for any kinda alcohol, but you go ahead and I'll toast you with a fresh cup of coffee."

As the men were preparing their toast, the big mountain man they met earlier approached their table. He doffed his hat to reveal a tousled head of black hair with a light frosting of grey, his dark complexion enabling him to pass as Indian, Mexican or even Negro but his bushy beard matched his hair and distracted Caleb from the man's coloring. His deep voice had a mellow ring to it as he said, "Pardon me folks, but the clerk down to the warehouse said you were the one in charge of that brigade headin' out in the mornin', is that right?"

"Yes, that's right," answered Caleb.

"My name's Beckwourth, Jim Beckwourth, and I was down at the Ring Tailed Tavern and this big man, I think they called him Bear, got into one whale of a fight, wrecked the whole place, cut up a couple fellas, and it took the Marshall and two deputies to finally get him outta there. Course the Marshall had to coldcock him with his pistol barrel to do it, but he's over in the jail now and I'm not sure the Marshall has any intention of lettin' him out."

"I'm not really surprised, that's what the man's known for, fightin' and wreckin' places. But I warned them all, if anybody got throwed in jail, they could rot, cuz I ain't bailin' 'em out," declared Caleb with a note of disgust in his voice. "But, have a seat Mr. Beckwourth, join us for a cup of coffee or if James here needs a drinkin' partner, he'd be glad to buy you a drink, I'm sure."

The rest of the evening was spent getting better acquainted with the well-known legend of the mountains. They shared their experiences with the Arapaho and Crow as Jim had married a woman of a different tribe of the Arapaho and also a woman of the Crow. Now his interest lay in the far West in California country. Although the gold rush of '49 was gaining steam, his interest was more in the money to be made off the miners and not the gold. As the company was breaking up, Jim asked Caleb, "So, if you're not goin' to get those men out, would it be all right with you if I bailed them out? I have need of a few more men for my next trip to the goldfields and your troublemakers might just fill the bill."

"Have at it Jim, as long as you know the kind of men they are and you're still willin' to give them a go, you have my blessing. To be honest, I'll be glad to be rid of 'em."

"Waaaghhhh, they ain't nothin' I can't handle. They ain't never seen the likes o'what this ol' coon can do. They try anything with me, I'll just lift their hair and leave 'em to the buzzards and tell everybody the Injuns done it!" he declared with a mischievous smile.

They parted with a handshake and a "Keep yore topknot on!" and Caleb and Clancy retired to the comfort of a feather bed and a night without setting a guard and hopefully a morning without the braying of mules. By the lantern light in their room, they talked about their future in the Medicine Bow and the sparkle returned to Clancy's eyes as she spoke of building their own cabin in the mountains. "And I want the front door facing the rising sun, I want to look out the window from my counter and see the first light of morning painting the grassy meadow below, and I want to see elk grazing below and I want to hear the bugle of a big bull elk again. Now, as far as them grizzlies are concerned though, you have to keep them away somehow."

"Now why should I do that? All you'd do is shoot 'em and use their claws for decoration like you did that other'n," he said with a smile as he picked up his wife in both arms and laid her gently on the feather mattress and watched her sink into the folds of the quilt and giggle.

IN THE EARLY MORNING LIGHT, THE COUPLE WALKED along the boardwalk enjoying the fresh new day before joining the men at the warehouse and corral. Looking down at the black ball of fur cradled in Clancy's arms, Caleb reached out and rubbed the pup's head and received a smile and an open mouth pant with a searching pink tongue in response. "So, what're ya' gonna call that thing, Two Bits Junior? He looks just like him, ya know."

"I'm not sure, I'm kinda waitin' to see what he becomes. I've thought of several, Rowdy, Rooster, Skipper, Digger, but I don't know yet. Maybe he'll find a name on his own," she thought aloud as she rubbed the pup behind his ears and let him lick her cheek.

Approaching the large corrals behind the warehouse, they noticed several of the men already busying themselves with the loading of the wagons. None of the wagons would be loaded heavy as their only cargo would be the necessary supplies for the men and trade goods for any friendly Indians and trappers they would meet on the way. In anticipation of bagging some buffalo as they crossed the plains, two of the wagons would be reserved for any early loads. Some of the men straggled in with obvious hangovers, but all quickly busied themselves and shared in the work. Before Caleb and Clancy drew near, a slight commotion stirred at the far end of the corral and Caleb stepped up on the fence to see what was happening. To his surprise, he saw the unmistakable bulk of Bear and his constant companion, Catman. He stepped down from the fence and turning to Clancy said, "You hang back a bit, I've got a problem to take care of."

"What is it, what's wrong?" she asked.

"It's Bear and Catman, they're back."

"But I thought that man, Beckwourth, was gonna take care of them?"

"Well, they came back here for something and I'm not sure I like it," he declared.

Approaching the group of men that were questioning Bear, Caleb pushed his way through to confront the big man. When Bear saw him he said, "Wal, here he is, the little whippersnapper his ownself. Now ain't he sumpin?"

"What are you doing here Bear? You heard what I said about gettin' in trouble."

"I don't care what you said, but you owe me some wages and I'm here to collect!"

"You already got all you had coming, just like the rest of the men. The rest comes in shares of the profits and you haven't made us any profit and you won't either, cuz you're no longer a part of this brigade!" declared Caleb firmly.

"Wal, if you ain't agonna pay up, then I'll just take it in supplies, an' you ain't gonna stop me cuz you ain't gotchor woman here to protect ya!" With a sneer and a grunt, he turned his back to Caleb to reach for some of the supplies that had just been loaded into the back of the wagon where they stood. As he stretched out an arm, he felt the tug on his shoulder and knowing it was Caleb, he started a roundhouse swing to flatten the leader of the brigade. But he was surprised when he pivoted to follow his swing and his massive fist met nothing but air. Caleb anticipated the swing and a step back allowed him to bring a haymaker from the ground and putting his entire weight behind the swing he buried his fist in the belly of the big man and was almost felled himself by the explosion of whiskey breath from the monster.

Quickly clasping his fists together, Caleb raised them over his head and brought the double fist down so fast it lifted his feet off the ground and pole-axed Bear behind the neck to take him to the ground. He stepped back and taking a deep breath he watched as the surprised Bear fought to lift himself from the dirt. "Don't do it! Let it be finished now," warned Caleb, but the big man, now up on all fours reached out in an attempt to snatch Caleb's leg from under him only to once again grab nothing but air. "Why'ntcha stand still and fight like a man?" bellowed the Bear as he stood to his feet. Then he let out a roar that matched his namesake and with arms outstretched he sought to capture the smaller man in his infamous bear hug that had won him so many battles before. Caleb waited until the last second, sidestepped and deftly tripped the onrushing mountain of a man who stumbled and caught himself on the sturdy wagon wheel. With another charge, he anticipated the move of Caleb and caught his buckskin with his outstretched paw and enveloped him in his massive arms with Caleb's arms pinned to his sides and began to squeeze the life out of the younger man. Caleb's face turned red as he gasped for air and facing the mass of whiskers and foul smelling breath he struggled to pull his head back, then closing his eyes he snapped his head forward and smashed the bulbous nose flat with his forehead in a splatter of blood that loosened the grasp and allowed Caleb to slip from his grip.

Staggering away from the bent over form of the massive mountain man, he watched as Bear put his hands to his face and came away with palms full of blood. Bear looked up at his prey and angrily roared again as he charged the still staggering Caleb. Feinting to the side, Caleb avoided the grasp and quickly pumped two solid blows to the right kidney as the attacker charged by. Bear whirled with surprising agility and balled up both fists and stepped forward bringing a swinging blow that glanced off the cheek of the retreating Caleb. The young man countered with an uppercut that carried his hundred ninety-five pounds behind it and parted his beard and snapped back the head of Bear. He staggered back with surprise written on his face and blood coming from his mouth. Caleb pursued with a flurry of punches to his midriff and his face. Bear was startled and overcome with the onslaught, staggering back into the waiting arms of Catman who thought to brace the big man but was knocked backwards as both men tumbled in a pile.

As the big man untangled himself he growled at Catman and as he stood erect, he swung at the smaller and only faithful partner he ever had, connected and Catman went to the ground unconscious. Turning to Caleb again he snarled, "Now I'm gonna beat you to death!"

Charging back into the fray, Bear expected to see fear on the face of the smaller man but was surprised to see determination and no give. As he neared Caleb, he growled again and started his swing, but Caleb easily ducked under and countered with another flurry of blows to his paunch that took the wind from the braggart and bully. As he started to bend over, Caleb standing directly in front of him snatched handfuls of the long hair over his ears, and as he pulled the big man's head down, he brought his leg up and smashed his face with his knee. Bear crumpled in a pile with blood coming from his nose, mouth and ears. With eyes now swollen and his lip split, he groaned as he struggled to rise again, but fell back on his face as Caleb bent over with hands on his knees and sucked air.

Clancy came to his side, put a hand on his back as he stood up and asked, "Are you all right? Then examining his reddened face, she added, "That's probably going to be quite the shiner you'll have come morning!"

Caleb nodded his head, stood erect and looked at Red and motioned for him and a couple others to drag the two men away from the wagons, and see them on their way. Red smiled with pride in his bourgeois and motioned for three more men to help him 'take out the trash'. As the rest of the crew cheerfully hitched up and loaded the wagons, it was just over an hour and all the wagons were ready, horses saddled and Reuben and his boys with fewer animals to handle motioned his readiness to depart. Caleb and Clancy, now mounted and lead rope in hand, waved at the waiting wagons and the brigade started moving westward.

The wagons lined out, each with a four-up hitch of mules, a mule-skinner up top and a helper beside him, followed by the herd of extra mules and horses. When the wagons returned with a full load of hides, they would be behind a six-up hitch, but until then the mules would be rotated and kept fresh. With ample horses for each of the hunters and skinners, the herd numbered almost sixty animals, and was well handled by Reuben and his well-trained boys.

Using the McCoy Campbell ferry that recently expanded to two ferries, the crossing of the Missouri River with wagons and animals was completed by midafternoon, leaving several hours of travel time. Caleb and Clancy resumed their scouting and hunting duties and preceded the train by at least a couple of miles. The chosen roadway was the beginning of the Oregon and Mormon trails, leaving Independence, crossing the Missouri above the junction with the Kansas, and bearing North West to eventually join the trail that followed the Platte River. This was the route marked out and used by many of the famous frontiersmen like Jim Bridger, Kit Carson, John Colter, Jedediah Smith and many others, some still living and working the wilderness. It would take at least a week for the brigade to reach the Platte and bear West to cross the great plains.

THE SIGNS OF THE SPREADING CIVILIZATION WERE scarring the landscape in every direction that Caleb gazed. Farmers were building homes with sandstone or sod, trees were becoming scarce as the same farmers were clearing and plowing the land. The trail the brigade followed had been widened by the increasing traffic of Mormons fleeing persecution in Missouri and elsewhere and following their leader's admonitions to go to their promised land in the West. Fremont's explorations of the West had instilled many with grand visions of adventure and riches to be had by any willing to make the journey. Caleb and Clancy Thompsett were not aware of the great movement under the flag of Manifest Destiny that was driving the political leaders of the East in a program of expansionism to extend the borders of a populated and civilized nation to the Pacific shores. What the young couple did see was the flow of settlers that spread like a massive colony of ants and was covering the land.

The two sat their horses atop a slight knoll that overlooked the broad horizon and gazed at the many plots of land now marked by the crooked rows of horse drawn plows. Smoke rose from mud-daubed chimneys of sod houses that blended with the surrounding countryside of buffalo grass and sage brush and nestled at the corner of rectangular patches of recently turned soil. Their expressions hid tumbling thoughts and questions but neither was voiced. Caleb turned to look behind them at the winding snake of disjointed wagons and mules and turned back to his wife and said, "We better be pushin' on, I'm thinkin' that over yonder," he spoke as he pointed with an extended arm and pointed finger that indicated a twisting stream lined with cottonwoods, ". . . might be a good place for camp." Then shading his eyes to look at the position of the sun, continued, "I figger we've made a good thirty miles and we still have an hour or more of daylight. So, it'll be an easy camp tonight. Yonder lies the Blue River, I'm thinkin', and we'll follow it North to the Platte. We're makin' good time," he surmised.

Less than half an hour brought them nearer the stream but spotting a thin wisp of smoke rising from the trees, they carefully approached. Caleb hailed, "Hello the camp! All right if we come in?"

A raspy voice responded from behind a nearby tree, "Only if'n' yore friendly, and keep yore hands away from any weapons or yore shore ta' lose 'em!" Slowly walking their horses forward, the couple saw two men lounging by the small campfire. Hanging from a green willow spit were bits of fresh meat broiling and dripping juices in the hot coals. One of the men was a wiry man with loose hanging and well soiled buckskins and sporting a mass of whiskers of grey that seemed to be fighting one another to escape their present predicament. A fur cap that appeared to be from a striped skunk sat at an angle held in place by a friar's row of shaggy grey hair that nestled over too small ears. Green eyes squinted at the visitors and a stream of tobacco juice missed its mark shy of the fire but the remains dribbled down the well-marked trail through the whiskers.

Seated next to him on the bark-less log was an Indian with fringed buckskin leggings, beaded moccasins, a breech cloth and bare-chested. Long braids of black with white frosting held bits of fur and feather for decoration to frame a stern expression from black eyes nestled under a single brow of black. Neither spoke but a voice came from the one that leaned against a tree at the edge of the camp, "We saw ya' comin' from up yonder on the hill. Ya shouldn't oughta skyline yourselves like that young'un. If'n I'd been of a mind, I mighta taken a shot atcha, just ta' see if'n I could still shoot that fer," then looking to Clancy and letting a broad smile try to escape from his tightly curled grey whiskers that bounced with every spoken word that came from his black skin framed mouth. His Negroid features were dominant with a broad nose that was often tickled by rogue whiskers, a dominant brow that did little to obscure his sparkling eyes that told of mischief, and a crown of short cropped grey thick curly hair. He dropped the butt of his Kentucky style long rifle to the ground and leaned on the muzzle as he looked at the red head. "Why ma'm, we're plumb pleased to welcome such a fine lookin' lady to our camp. Step down and join us fer supper, we got plenty to share." Then turning to Caleb, he added, "And you too, sonny."

Caleb stepped down, took the pup from his wife and stepped back as she swung a leg over the rump of her horse and dropped to the ground. Handing the pup back to his wife he turned to look at the men and began to explain, "We're leadin' a buffalo brigade and they'll be along shortly. We're scoutin' a campsite for them and thought along through here would be a good site but we don't want to impose on you fellas, so we can move a bit downstream if you don't mind?" he asked.

"A buffler brigade? Now I've heard of ever'thin', I knowed 'bout trappin' brigades, but ain't ne'er heard 'bout no buffler brigade."

"Well, we just started callin' it that cuz we're just goin' after buffalo, since there's not much market for beaver. The Chouteau company outfitted us and we're headin' to the country along the Oregon Trail past Fort John."

"Oh, you mean Fort Laramie, they done changed the name of it when the army moved in. Ya ever been out thataway, sonny?"

"I've been through there a couple of times," then looking at the men he added, "Aren't you old timers a long way from the mountains?"

"Wal, like you said, there ain't much market fer beaver and the load of plews we just took to Independence didn't bring us much and we was just a palaverin' 'bout what we was gonna do when we saw you two up on that thar hillside."

Caleb and Clancy accepted the outstretched cups of coffee and seated themselves on a large boulder to the side of the campfire. Caleb smiled at his bride and turned to the men and started, "Maybe I can help with that. We lost a couple of our hunters back in Independence and we just happen to need a few more. Course, I'm not sure you old timers can handle a trip like that, cuz you know we'd be going through some Indian country and your scalps might be mighty tempting, and I don't know if you fellas could still see far enough to hit anything with those old long toms you're packin'" said Caleb, trying to keep a straight face. "And then there's that Injun there, just havin' him along might make some of those other bands unhappy with us, havin' one of their enemies with us."

The reclining oldster jumped to his feet and snatched off his fur cap as he said, "Now you listen hyar you young whippersnapper, you ain't seen the day you kin keep up with us and we could drop two or three buffler while you're still figgerin' out how to pull the trigger. And as fer them Injuns," pointing at his bald head, "ain't no Injun out there gonna scalp me agin!"

With that the black mountain man stepped forward and added as he pointed at the still immobile Indian, "Sides, he ain't no Injun. That thar is Pedro Garcia and he just wishes he was a Injun!"

The skinny mountain man lifted his gaze and looked back at Caleb as he said, "I reckon that's yore outfit comin' now," with a nod of his head at the distant hilltop. "Go 'head on and have 'em circle up yonder, just keep yore animals downstream of us. I ain't interested in makin' coffee with tainted water." As the wagons approached, Caleb walked out from the trees and waved the train to circle up in the clearing adjacent to the cottonwoods.

The following morning as they were lining out, the three original campers moved their mounts alongside Caleb and the bigger man said, "Wal, we done decided we'd tag along a ways and see if'n you can keep up with us old-timers. By the way, I'm called Rooster, that thar is Bones and the Indian is Chicken. We call him that cuz he wanted us to call him Soaring Eagle but he warn't no good at soaring, just snorin', so we just call him chicken cuz when he's snorin', he squawks!" Caleb turned to look at the stoic face of the big black man and smiled with a chuckle and added, "Glad to have you with us, but now you've got to earn your pay."

"Pay, you mean we're gettin' paid fer this outin'?"

"Every shooter gets a dollar a day plus a share in the take," declared the brigade leader.

"Hey, ya hear that fellers? We're gettin' paid! Now ain't that some shinin'! So, whatcha want us to be a doin' fer all this hyar money?"

"Well, these fellas get pretty hungry, so how 'bout you three head off on your own and see if you can make meat. Anything you get, just hang 'side the trail and Cooky'll pick it up and have it sizzlin' by the time you get back into camp."

"Now that sounds like a purty good deal. You got it!" declared the big man as he reined his mount to the side and waved his compatriots to join him in the hunt.

Three more days of travel saw fewer farms and less of civilization's encroachment. Before the morning sun crested the distant flat line horizon, Caleb and company were finishing the morning coffee as he turned to the three newcomers and said, "How 'bout you fellas splittin' up this mornin' and take a couple of these greenhorns under your wing and see if you can't teach them a few things about the country?"

"Waaaghhh, now you want us to nursemaid some of these pilgrims?"

"Not nursemaid, just share your wealth of wilderness knowledge," replied Caleb leaning heavily on the flattery. "You know, all that great wisdom you have garnered with your vast experience, just share it a little. I've got a couple of young fellas that are ripe for the teaching." He waved over Colton and Chance Threet, the two cotton topped brothers that were the last ones to join up in St. Louis. As the brothers neared the fire, the old timers eyed the book-end young men standing before them. With broad shoulders, tapered waists, well-muscled arms and thick necks that held smiling and enthusiastic faces, the boys were men with youthful smiles. The old-timers chimed in together as they said, "Now them's some purty big fellers, they might be some help after all," as they reached to squeeze the sizable biceps of the young men.

"Also, I'm sure I don't need to tell you, but yesterday we saw a trio of young bucks, Pottawatomi I think, but they just looked us over and I don't think they'll be any trouble. But just keep your eyes peeled."

"Yup, and in this neck of the woods, ya' might watch fer some o' them Kickapoo. Usually they're friendly, but ya never can tell. I think they got 'em a village over yonder a ways," shared Bones.

"If you spot any buffalo, enough to make a stop worthwhile, come back and let the train know cuz some of these fellas that are 'sposed to be shooters ain't never taken a buffalo and you might school 'em a bit," instructed Caleb. The two groups of hunters, Rooster with Chance and Bones and Chicken with Colton, went to opposite sides of the trail as Caleb and Clancy followed the rutted and winding wagon trail on their scout.

THE CROSSING OF THE PLATTE RIVER PROVED TO BE more of a challenge than Caleb anticipated. With recent rains farther upstream the water level was higher and the current was moving faster than usual. Although even at high water, the broad Platte appeared to be nothing more than slow moving thick mud, and that was deceptive. Harboring deep eddies of quicksand, sandbars that appeared solid but gave way with the first track, submerged snags of trees and constantly eroding banks, the Platte claimed more than its share of lives and livestock.

The caravan approached the wide crossing where the Platte split into two less forbidding streams with the first providing the greater challenge. Caleb sat in his saddle with both hands on the pommel and stretched up to get a better look at the stream below. Clancy watched her man and looked at the river before them and said, "It doesn't look too bad, we've crossed faster streams."

"Yeah, but they had rocky crossings and you could see the bottom. You could pick your way across, but this is like wading through a mud puddle. " He sat back in his saddle and pondered. *Now, I remember us crossin' this river with the wagon train when Scratch and us came out West before, but it weren't this bad. What if we get one o' them wagons stuck in there?* A smile crossed his face and Clancy knew he had his solution or at least an idea for accomplishing the crossing. He turned to his mate and said, "Let's go on across and we'll look at the other branch and see what it's like."

The deepest part of the river barely touched the bellies of the horses and pack mule as the couple gave the horses their heads and let them pick their way across. Caleb eyed what appeared to be a whirlpool slightly downstream and made a mental note to warn the others of the hazard. Their horses confidently picked their way across and were soon stepping on the sandbar and started their usual rolling shake to rid themselves of the excess water. Clancy laughed at the terrified look her pup gave her as he sat between her and the pommel of the saddle. When she laughed and rubbed his head, the pup relaxed and with open mouth let his tongue show his smile at his companion. He squirmed like he wanted to stretch his legs and Clancy bent low cradling the pup with her hand under his belly and dropped him the rest of the way to the ground. He took off on an exploratory tour of the wide sandbar and soon disappeared into some scrub brush. Both Caleb and Clancy laughed at the antics of the pup and Caleb asked, "Have you decided on a name for that rascal?"

"I think so, he's always wantin' to run and get in trouble, kinda like you, so I think I'll call him Rowdy," she said with a smile to her husband.

"Rowdy, hummm? Yeah, that suits him," replied Caleb as he watched the pup searching the low lying brush on the wide sandbar that resembled a large island. Rowdy trotted toward a cluster of cottonwood intermingled with gooseberry bushes, flushed out a cottontail to his surprise and the bewildered dog sat back on his haunches to watch the rabbit disappear into the brush. "He sure is growin' fast, pretty soon he'll be too big to ride with you," observed Caleb. Clancy found a shady recluse by the cottonwood, sat on a piece of driftwood and called Rowdy to her side. Rubbing the dog behind his ears, she watched as Caleb crossed back to the South side of the river to await the mule train.

As the first wagon, driven by Don Brown, arrived he signaled for them to hold in place until all the wagons were lined out and the herd gathered nearby. Caleb walked to Reuben's side and instructed him to harness a four up team and take them across the river and wait. Returning to Don's side as he stood by his wagon where the other muleskinners had assembled, Caleb explained his plan and cautioned the muleskinners about the whirlpool and quicksand just downstream of their crossing.

Mid-morning saw seven wagons across the first branch of the Platte and the lead wagons starting across the second and smaller branch. Reuben sat on a large piece of driftwood anchored in the deep sand as he held the leads of the four-up team that rested hip-shot in the morning sun. Each wagon would cross slightly upstream of the preceding wagon to ensure at least the upstream wheels had solid footing undisturbed by the wagon before it and the crossing of the wagons was progressing smoothly.

But when the wagon under the guidance of the big German, Johannes Weinfort, chose to follow the route of the first wagon and soon bogged down in the loose silt. He stood in the wagon box and cracked a long bullwhip over the heads of the four up team of mules that were leaning into their traces and struggling to find solid footing. The more they pulled, the deeper the broad wheels of the freighter dug into the mud while the incessant yelling and whip-cracking of the muleskinner contributed to the stumble of the left lead mule that scrambled for footing, sunk to its neck and panicked for air.

Reuben quickly responded and brought the four-up harnessed team to the edge of the water, grabbed the long tow rope and waded to the struggling mules. As he reached the team, he sought to settle them down as he spoke, but the crack of the bull-whip from Johannes just over his head caused him to yell at the muleskinner, "You do that agin' an' I'll rip that from yo hands and beatchu wid it!"

The German coiled his whip and as he dropped the coil and started his backswing, Reuben focused on the mules and reached between them to run his tow rope through the metal clevis at the end of the wagon tongue. Securing the tow rope, he stood and signaled the young man waiting with the team on the sandbar to start the pull. With the extra team digging in and adding to the pull, the encouragement from Reuben by the side of the bogged down team, and the slapping leads on their rumps, the mules leaned into their traces and the wagon was soon freed.

With the wagon on solid ground, Reuben leaned in and loosed the tow rope to free the extra team. As he stood and turned he faced the big German who stood with feet wide spread and the bull whip hanging by his side. The broad shouldered blonde haired and bearded German growled at Reuben and said, "Vaht did you say you vud do wit me?" he snarled in a challenge to the former stevedore.

"Ain't nobody eber gonna lay a whip to me, ever agin!" answered Reuben as he flexed his fists and spoke through clenched teeth.

The big blonde flipped the end of his whip behind him, extended his left arm toward the black man and brought the black snake forward in a flashing arc searching for flesh to rip. Without moving from his stance, and without cutting his gaze away from the red eyes of the German, Reuben grabbed the whistling leather tongue from the air, wrapped his arm with one loop and jerked the German off his feet. The surprised muleskinner fought to stand as the angry Reuben approached swinging the handle of the bull whip in a taunting and threatening manner. When the big eyed German stood watching the rippling muscles in the chest of Reuben, he stepped back and stuttered, "Vh . . vh. . vhait, I... I ! "

Reuben said, "I'se tempted ta use dis on you, but I

swore on my momma's memry, I'd never let anyone use one of dese on 'nother man. So, yo gonna hafta learn ta' drive dem mules wit'out dis. " Standing within inches of the big German, Reuben scowled and said, "Let 'dis be da last of it and get that wagon movin'!"

Clancy watched the entire confrontation and as the German turned away from Reuben and climbed on his wagon, she let her breath escape and realized she had been frozen breathless all the while. She smiled at herself and at the response of the big black stevedore. Caleb had spoken highly of the man and Reuben had always been very respectful of her and she nodded her head as she thought of the suggestion of Caleb to, ". . . ask Reuben to come with them to the ranch."

With all the wagons now on solid ground, Caleb lined them out on the trail that would follow the North bank of the Platte for the bulk of their journey. The staggered landings had enabled the men to grab their noon meal of left-over biscuits and thin sliced deer steaks as time allowed and the remainder of the day would see the caravan making up lost time. Caleb was thankful as he realized the rest of the trail held few river crossings and none as challenging as those already conquered. The way before them would be mostly tall grass prairie with plenty of trees, brush, and ample game for the travelers. With the designated hunters providing plenty of meat with deer, antelope and an occasional bear with numerous rabbits and turkeys, the caravan traveled with full stomachs and smiling faces. The old mountain men reported seeing a few Indians but always in the distance and none appeared threatening. The Sauk, Fox, and Otoe were the tribes that frequented the Platte River flats West of the Missouri, but all were considered friendly and posed no concern for the brigade.

Four days of easy travel through the wide valley beside the Platte put many miles behind them and now as he watched the setting sun use the palette of clouds to paint a panorama of varying shades of orange and gold, Caleb thanked his God for another good day. They were camped near the river in a large grove of ancient cottonwoods that towered over the tangle of willows and chokecherry at their base. It was a comfortable camp and the couple was seated together on a rotted log adjacent to their small cook fire. They were enjoying the visit from the two old-timers that shared the tales of their youth and time as trappers.

As Bones was spinning a tale of their time in the Absaroka Mountains and a run-in with a Crow hunting party, he told about a young woman that was a war-leader, "She was a fearsome one, she was. Weren't never a brave that could out-do that female wolf in any kinda fight, nosiree, Bob. I tell you, when we saw she was a leadin' that bunch, we tucked tail and skedaddled on outta there and we didn't let no grass grow under our feet, I'ma sayin.'"

Caleb and Clancy looked at one another and chuckled a mite before Bones asked, "Now what's so all fired funny 'bout that? I tol' you the straight of it, and we come so close to losin' our hair, that's what made me go bald, just the fear of that female takin' it with a knife!"

Caleb stifled his laughter as he asked, "Was that woman warrior the one they call Pine Leaf?"

The startled look on the old man's face was quickly replaced with a scowl, "You know, I believe it was, least-ways that's what I heeerd anyhows, yeah, Pine Leaf. Ain't that right Rooster?" he asked his partner and received an enthusiastic shake of his head in answer. Both men looked at Caleb with a question written across their face when Rooster chimed in, "And how would you know 'bout that, young'un?"

With a broad smile at Clancy, Caleb looked to the oldtimers and answered, "She's my Ma's best friend and the wife of my Uncle, Broken Shield," and he continued to explain, "When she ran up against a Blackfoot war party and my Pa and Shield pitched in and brought her out of the fight, Shield nursed her back to life and ended up marryin' her. Now he's the leader of the Northern band of Arapaho and she's there right alongside him. Their marriage brought a truce between the Crow and the Arapaho."

"Wal, if I ain't a dung eatin' beetle, an' here we thot you was some kinda tenderfoot an' you been holdin' out on us all this time," and turning to Rooster the old man said, "I guess that makes us buzzard bait on this ol' prairie, don't it Rooster? We done been hornswaggled!" declared the mountain man as he looked at the couple with new respect.

As the rising sun lanced the morning with shafts of gold, the bright rays of light warmed the backs of the muleskinners as the wagons rolled along the dusty trail. The low rambling hills held promise with each crest that obscured the road beyond. The anticipation of discovery of new vistas and adventure led the travelers as the terrain slowly changed from the tall green grasses that waved as they passed and handed them off to the towering elm, maple and oak trees that proliferated along the well-watered valley, to the browns and dark greens of sandstone and juniper and pinion trees. As they turned the page of this new chapter of travel the men of the brigade took in the rim-rocked plateaus and mesas and the flats with low growing buffalo grass. Caleb and Clancy were vigilant as Caleb had cautioned his companion about the possibility of buffalo appearing in great numbers. His words were no sooner cataloged than the next bend of the trail around a small knob revealed a mass of brown moving in cadence to a rumbling roar beneath a large cloud of dust that left a trail that drifted to the distant hills.

The couple reined up and sat mesmerized at the mass of woolies that plodded along with their ground eating gait with heads slowly swinging side to side and an undercurrent of sound that could easily be interpreted as conversation between the animals. Extending as far as they could see in both directions, the couple marveled at the mass of monsters before them. With yearlings of lighter color bouncing along and playfully kicking up their heels, the mothers would occasionally swing wide and nudge the youngsters back in line with a gentle but firm butt of the bulbous head and a bellow of admonition. The bigger bulls were at the forefront and the older slower moving animals would be bringing up the rear. The dust cloud slowly drifted to encompass the watching couple as Clancy held firmly to the scruff of the neck of Rowdy as he stood with paws on the pommel and occasionally barking at the passing herd.

"Let's head back to the wagons and let 'em know what we found. This herd will be passing for hours so we got lots of time," but as he reined his horse around he paused and looking at Clancy he added, ". . . tell you what. How 'bout you takin' the pack mule and goin' back to the wagons and tell 'em what's up and I'll go round up the old timers and the boys. I'll meetcha back here in a little bit." Clancy smiled and nodded her head as she reached for the lead rope of the pack mule, put her heels to her mount and parted with a "See ya."

Caleb kicked his mount up to a ground eating canter and angled off to the North East to find the hunters that rode on the flank of the mule train. He knew they would be riding along the shoulder of the nearby rim rock mesas that held many timber lined draws that were refuges for deer and antelope and it surprised Caleb when he spotted his hunters standing behind a cluster of juniper with their mounts beside them. Suspecting they were stalking some game, he let out a mimicry of the red-tailed hawk to get their attention. Still almost a hundred yards distant, the hunters saw the approaching Caleb and motioned him to drop down below the nearby shoulder of the ridge. He quickly dismounted, surveyed the nearby terrain and slowly led his horse as he walked to the hunters. As he approached, they motioned for him to look to his left. He turned, saw nothing, tiptoed, again nothing and ground tying his mount he bellied up to the crest of the slight knoll. Between two and three hundred yards distant and sitting just below the top of a ridge was a party of Indian warriors, about fifteen, watching the dust cloud of the retreating buffalo.

Returning to his mount, he joined his hunters. Bones, Colton and Chicken watched as their young leader approached. Bones greeted him with, "How many ya' reckon?"

"Looks like about fifteen, but they're all warriors 'though not painted. I make 'em out to be Pawnee, whatchu think?" asked Caleb deferring to the more experienced mountain man.

"Yup, yore right 'bout that and this is shore 'nuff Pawnee country. Whatcha figger they be lookin' at?"

"There's a big herd of buffalo headin' for water yonder. They're probably waitin' for 'em to stop at the river."

"Well, if that's all there be of 'em, we kin handle 'em, but if they got the rest of their village waitin' back yonder, we might be in a bit of a pickle," observed Bones.

"You know; this is somethin' that's been naggin' at me ever since I took this job. I know there's been some hide hunters that just kill ever thing they see, take the hides and leave the rest to rot while some Indian villages go hungry. Just don't seem right somehow."

With a pensive stare the old mountain man said, "I recomember back when we first started trappin' they wuz so many beaver it seemed like we'd never run short. But ya' know, it didn't take long fer it ta' git ta' wheres we had to go farther an' farther up inta them shinin' mountains to find even a few o' them furbellies. Now with more n' more o' these hyar buffalo brigades, I'm a thinkin' the same things gonna happen with the woolies, yessir I do."

Nodding his head in agreement with the old timer, Caleb turned to Chicken and Colton and said, "You two wait here and watch. If we don't come back you can take a warning to the mule train, but don't follow us, understand?" Chicken grunted his response and Colton nodded his head. "C'mon Bones, let's go talk to some Injuns," ordered the young bourgeois.

As they neared the hunting party, Caleb and Bones approached with left hands holding the reins and right hands uplifted with open palms in the common sign for peace. The stoic Pawnee watched as the two men neared. Most of the warriors had the traditional Mohawk roach with feathers trailing down their backs. Most were bare chested while some had the traditional bone breast plate while others had beaded buckskin vests. All wore fringed leggings and breechcloths. Some held lances with most bearing beaded quivers bristling with arrows for the bows that rested beside the quivers. Two had smooth bore fusils. Curious and distrustful eyes followed the two white men as they came alongside their leader. Caleb broke the stalemate with a greeting of *Nowa*. The leader tried to hide his surprise but answered, *Nowa*.

Caleb was proficient with sign language and he used it while he spoke in English to introduce himself and Bones. Caleb told of coming this way before and their time spent with the Pawnee after another buffalo hunt. He told of the time of the *Taaka Pii'ta* or Medicine Buffalo when his friend Scratch had told Spotted Horse about the great medicine and the feast they shared. Then Caleb asked about Spotted Horse. The leader of the band, Walks with Clouds, said his brother, Spotted Horse had gone to the other side. Caleb asked, "Are you looking for *ta'raha'*?" With a quick nod and his lance extended in the direction of the dust cloud Walks with Clouds said they would take buffalo from that herd.

"We are hunting buffalo also and we have many hunters but we will take mostly the hides and there will be plenty buffalo for your village. If you send for your women and others, we will kill the buffalo and you can have most of the meat."

"We can kill our own *ta'raha'*!" proclaimed Walks with Clouds.

"Yes, you are all great hunters, but we have these," he said as he pulled his Sharps from the scabbard. He stepped down from his horse and dropped to one knee, he had spotted a lone wolf that was shadowing the herd before they stopped to talk to the Indians, and he searched the distant hillside for the wolf. Catching a movement as the dark grey lobo walked slowly just below the ridge, he estimated the distance at five hundred yards, adjusted his rear peep sight, set the rear trigger and drew a bead on the distant target. The still mounted Indians shielded their eyes to watch the slow moving wolf and looked at the shooter then to the wolf again. As Caleb drew breath, let some escape, he slowly squeezed the trigger. The explosion from the Sharps startled Indian and horses alike as all the horses snapped their heads up and the paint mare beside Walks with Clouds jumped back like his legs were tightly coiled springs and when his feet hit the ground again, he dropped his head between his legs and arched his back and bucked down the hillside, losing his rider on the second hop. The remaining Indians broke out in excited chatter as some laughed at the now humbled rider that chased after his horse while others pointed to the downed wolf as they gestured at Caleb and his rifle.

"Do all your hunters have rifles like this?" asked Walks with Clouds.

"All the hunters have rifles, but not all like this. If you join us in this hunt, I will let you shoot a *ta'raha'* with this," stated Caleb as he lifted his rifle before him.

Walks with Clouds dispatched two of his men to the village while the remainder followed Caleb, Bones and Walks with Clouds to the designated meeting place with the mule train. The approaching party of Indians had most of the men apprehensive even with Bones and Caleb in the lead, but after explanations were given, the shooters gathered by the lead wagon for instructions from their leader.

Dividing the hunters in groups to be commanded by

Bones, Rooster, Red and two other selected leaders, Caleb cautioned the men on their approach and shooting. "We're not gonna take more'n four or five each, and we'll keep the meat from maybe eight of 'em and the rest of the meat's goin' to Walks with Clouds and his people. They'll be takin' some animals too, but the best part is, his women'll do most of the skinnin' and butcherin' and that's a good opportunity for all y'all to learn how it's done the right way. So, when they start in, you be there ta' help 'em and get some schoolin'."

The hunt went well with over fifty buffalo taken by the brigade and a good dozen more by the Indians. With the Indians riding in among the Buffalo, the shooters had to watch their aim, but none were hurt. When Caleb let Walks shoot his Sharps, the chief was startled and surprised at the kick from the "shoots far" rifle, but immediately tried unsuccessfully to trade Caleb out of the rifle. Shooters and skinners alike worked with the women as the skinning and butchering was begun. The inexperienced buffalo hunters were amazed at the size of the beasts from close-up and especially surprised at the difficulty in skinning the carcass and removing it from under the beasts. But when the women pushed aside the steaming pile of guts and sliced the raw liver, dipped the pieces in the bile and bit into the slices, some of the men lost their breakfast while others partook of the treat. When the women showed them how to start the hide, use a horse to pull it loose, roll over the carcass, and finish peeling the wooly coat, the men appreciated the lesson in expedience.

It was well into the night when the work was done

under the watchful gaze of a full moon but several of the women had already started searing buffalo steaks on nearby fires and willingly shared the feast with the brigade.

The grey light of early morn saw the retreat of the Pawnee with the women walking beside several horses trailing travois laden with mounds of meat as they disappeared into a narrow defile between two rim rock ridges that marked a flat mesa. The mule train was lined out and continuing on their trek West with the herd of mules and horses trailing behind. The brigade now had a different outlook on their adventure, with optimistic thoughts about a successful hunt and the profit sharing bounty that awaited their return.

Caleb waved the mule train away from the trail to make an early camp. Rooster had chosen the site as discussed with Caleb and they considered the need for a site that provided ample willows and chokecherry for the needed task. With the abundance of fresh buffalo, the experienced mountain men knew much of the meat would need to be smoked to prevent spoilage and smoking required certain woods and ample time. Caleb, Clancy with Rooster and Chance had already cut many willows and chokecherry for making the smoking racks and providing the right smoke for the meat. As the wagons circled up, Caleb began giving directions to those not otherwise occupied with the usual camp duties. Three men dropped the tailgates of wagons and began cutting the meat into narrow strips while others began assembling the drying racks under the tutelage of Clancy. Two men were dispatched to find dry hardwoods to make the beds of coals over which the racks would suspend the strips of meat. Other men pitched in to help and learn and a line of six fires were soon flaring to begin the process. The fires would need to be tended through the night as the smoking of the meat would take several hours.

The men alternated shifts at the smoke racks while several took their breaks for the evening meal of thick and juicy buffalo steaks and Dutch oven beans and biscuits. Caleb sat his tin plate and cup down, stood and walked to the edge of the circle of wagons, lifted a foot to rest on the tongue of one and looked out across the flats to the nearby mesas now casting long shadows. As Clancy walked to her husband's side she asked, "What is it? What's bothering you?"

"Oh, it's probably nothin' but Bones and Colton and Chicken haven't come in. They know we don't need any meat but Bones was lookin' for some yams and rose hips and other such like. Said he was tired of beans. Hard tellin' what he'll come up with, but I don't think he'll get into too much trouble."

Rooster noticed the two looking beyond the wagons and walked up behind them and asked, "Lookin' fer Bones are ye?"

Caleb turned to the old timer, nodded his head and turned back to the distant shadows. "Yeah, we're just gettin' into Sioux country and they're not apt to be too friendly, like the Pawnee."

"Yore sure right 'bout that. Them red devils is the worst enemies them Pawnee have and they shore don't like any white man bein' in their huntin' grounds. I only got into one scrape with them blood thirsty devils and I purt' near didn't make it. Thot shore I was gonna wake up lookin' down on them clouds. But ol' Bones ain't no tenderfoot, he can take care hisself," reassured the old timer. Caleb looked at him, nodded his head and with his arm loosely draped over Clancy's shoulder, they returned to the fire.

They were no sooner seated when a distant gunshot brought them to their feet, another sounded soon after and the thunder of hooves and shouted war cries gave the alarm to the brigade. "Get your rifles and take cover!" shouted Caleb and he and Clancy snatched their rifles from the log nearby and ran to the circle of wagons. Taking up position at the corner of the wagon they just left, Clancy dropped to one knee and looked under the elbow of her standing husband. "There!" she shouted as she pointed to three horses charging straight toward them. Laying low on their mounts necks were Bones, Colton and Chicken as they whipped the mounts toward the refuge of the mule train. Less than twenty yards behind them was a band of screaming Indians slowly gaining in the chase. Caleb took quick aim, set the trigger and squeezed off the first shot, dropping the paint pony head over heels and launching its rider to land flat on his back and without chance to prevent being trampled to death by the other pursuing mounts. Clancy and Rooster also shot with another horse felled and another warrior dropped from his mount. Several other shots sounded but the charging Indians turned away from the gunfire and moved to a slight sagebrush covered knoll to regroup. Bones and company were motioned into the circle, dropped from their mounts and upon seeing Rooster and Caleb, Bones said, "Well, looks like we got us a real shindig lined up. Sorry boss, I didn't invite them rascals, they just come of their own accord!"

"How many ya reckon there are?" asked Caleb

"Ain't shore, didn't think to stop an' count 'em, what with them not actin' too friendly and all. But I don't think thems the only ones. We cut track on a bigger bunch and I think they mighta split up, so I don't rightly know how many there be."

Caleb looked to Rooster, back at Bones and said, "Any ideas?"

"Well, we got us a purty good set-up rightchere, so I'm thinkin' we need to just wait 'em out. If we took off, with it gettin' dark soon we shore couldn't outrun 'em with these hyar wagons, so I vote we just sit an' wait," drawled Rooster. Bones shook his head in agreement and Clancy just looked to her man for his decision. He looked in the direction of the distant Sioux and said, "Well, Rooster you work your way over yonder," pointing to the far right of the semi-circle of the wagons, "and Bones you take that side," nodding to the left arc of wagons. The herd of horses and mules were between the wagons and the river and Caleb thought the river would be a detriment to any attackers and felt safe with their backs protected, but decided caution would be best observed. He assigned Colton and Chicken to station themselves to each side of the herd and to watch for any attackers that might try for the herd from the river. The men had no sooner taken their places when the whisper of arrows caught Caleb's attention and he looked up to see a hailstorm of arrows arcing over the wagons and seeking targets of flesh. He yelled, "Duck for cover, arrows!" and stepped to the end of the wagon and shielded his woman with his body. With a grunt, Caleb stumbled slightly as an arrow buried itself in his shoulder blade and another creased his side. "I think we found the rest of the war party," he said to his wife. He watched in the direction of the arrow launch while his wife continued her vigil of the retreating warriors. She shouted, "Here they come!"

"Hold your fire . . . hold . . .hold . . ." as the charging Indians neared with each warrior laying low on the neck of his mount, ". . . fire!" The barrier of lead and smoke greeted the charging horde with death as horses and warriors alike dug trenches of dirt, sand and rocks as bloody bodies were splattered across the bare plains before the wagons. The brigade had been cautioned to stagger their shots so there would always be shooters and now those that had held their fire let loose with a second volley that felled most of the remaining warriors. Three warriors reined their mounts to the side, dropped to the opposite sides of their mounts with one leg hooked over the back and an arm over the neck, they fled the deadly fire.

Screams from the left side of the arc of wagons brought the men around in time to see another horde of attackers climbing over the wagons to attack the defenders furiously trying to reload their rifles. Both Caleb and Clancy brought their pistols to bear and repeatedly fired dropping several of the attackers from the wagons even though Clancy's attention was drawn to the arrow protruding from her husband's back. The brief reprieve allowed the men to complete their reloads and the men of the brigade rallied to the side of the defenders and repelled the attack. Several red bodies were draped on the tall sideboards of the wagons and over the tongues that separated the freighters. The ground before the arc bore the signs of the first attack with the carcasses of horses and Indians alike. The grisly scene was soon silenced as the shroud of death touched attacker and defender alike.

Clancy made her husband sit on the tongue of the wagon as she examined the wound in his back and said, "Hold on to that footboard, this is gonna hurt!" Caleb took a grip on the protruding board, bent slightly to give his wife better access and gritted his teeth and said, "Go." Putting her knee beside the arrow and both hands on the shaft she pulled with no success. "That's stuck in your shoulder blade, I'll have to wiggle it free, hold on." With that brief warning, she again placed her knee and began her work. She wrenched the arrow free to the relief and gasp of her husband. Quickly packing the wound with the torn off end of a neck scarf, she said, "It's gonna hurt, but you'll be O.K."

Caleb walked behind the members of the brigade and cautioned them to stay alert for another attack. Cooky and his helper, Lazarus, were tasked with tending to the wounded and they set up their make shift hospital by one of the freighters nearest the herd of horses. When the count was taken, there were two dead and five others wounded, but Rooster had counted at least sixteen dead and many more wounded among the Sioux. Rooster and Bones joined Caleb where the young man stood watch as dusk dropped across the prairie. "I think they've decided it's too costly to keep up this fight. If we drag them bodies away from the circle a mite, they'll probably disappear in the night and we can head out in the morning," observed Rooster.

"Yeah, I think you're right. If they don't have to come any closer'n that for the bodies, I think they'll just take 'em an' leave," agreed Caleb. Looking at the two older men he added, "I think these pilgrims did a pretty good job in their first fight, don'tchu?" Both men grinned and nodded their heads in agreement. Bones added, "Yup, these men'll do to ride the river with, by gum, yessiree."

Under the watchful eyes of several men stationed and ready at the edge of the circle, four others dragged the many bodies about twenty yards from the mule train and returned without any sign of the remaining Sioux. As expected, when daylight came the only carcasses left on the prairie were the downed horses. When full light spread across the plains, the mule train was well on its way toward the distant land mark of Courthouse Rock.

CLANCY SAT ON THE LARGE BOULDER WITH ELBOWS on knees looking at the trail that stretched back into the narrow valley the brigade recently exited. She let her mind travel back the many years past when she was with her Mum and Da traveling with the wagon train. She remembered asking her Mum about the formations of Courthouse Rock, Chimney Rock and Scotts Bluff and how her Mum explained the erosion of time and the slow changes wrought by wind and rain.

"Everything changes darlin', maybe someday you'll see this again and it will be different than today. And it's the same way with people, one day your Da and I will be gone, you'll be a woman with your own family and life will go on but different, changed you know?" The trip down memory lane brought a melancholy mood and she picked up a rock and chucked it at a patch of cactus, looked beyond the rocks to the rich bottomland and remembered. She saw herself running through the willows along the riverbank with Two Bits, her big shaggy black dog and constant companion, chasing after her. She spotted a fleeing cottontail and gave chase swatting the willows with her staff and giggling as the bunny hopped to the next cluster. It was a fun time and a fond memory.

The sudden blast of a gunshot broke her reverie as she jerked and looked toward the nearby copse of cottonwood. Caleb had disappeared into the trees stalking a flock of turkeys as he carried the borrowed Holland and Holland double barreled shotgun. Cooky had bragged on the shotgun to Caleb and willingly let the younger man put it to the test. Another blast from the shotgun brought Clancy to her feet as she searched the thick trees and brush for some sign of her man. She heard the flutter of wings as the flock of turkeys took flight but a double blast from the shotgun made the flight of two birds come to a quick end. Clancy smiled as she knew her husband had been successful with his hunt for a little variety to their fare.

She led the horses toward the copse of trees as her husband exited the grove with the shotgun slung over his shoulder and carrying two handsful of grey and black feathers with wings flopping wide. He lifted one high and with a broad smile said, "Well, I got Cooky some birds for the pot! That shotgun's pretty handy, I might have to get one." He walked to the pack mule and stuffed the birds in one of the panniers and spoke over his shoulder to his wife, "Ya want me to save one for our fire?"

"Well, that depends on how early we'll be stopping. If we get to the fort early enough, I can put one on a spit over the fire and make a good meal, but if we're not gonna get there too soon, it'd be best to let Cooky put 'em in his pot."

He turned to face his wife and as he lowered the shotgun, he grimaced as his shoulder reminded him of his recent wound. Clancy noticed and said, "That flint tipped arrow left a reminder in your shoulder blade but Cooky chipped the sharp edge off so you should heal up pretty good, but like I told you, it'll be sore for a while." The attack was four days past and his wound was healing, but the tenderness to the touch and soreness of the muscle would take longer. "Yeah, I know, but fortunately it's my left shoulder and not my shootin' arm. But we should make the fort before dusk, we'll see. Maybe we need to keep an eye out for some additions to the pot, maybe some cat tail root, yams, onions, and such, ya reckon?"

"Yeah, I've eaten enough beans on this trip to last a lifetime!" answered the smiling Clancy.

The two mounted up and continued their scout for the mule train. Today would be an easy day of travel with the usual ups and downs of the rolling hills but the terrain had flattened out pretty well and the mules were not facing any challenges for the pull. The couple often spent their time together sharing thoughts and ideas regarding their future home in the Medicine Bow basin at the foot of the Medicine Bow range. Clancy broke the silence of their contemplation with "I'm glad that the Threet brothers are coming with us, they're good boys."

"Boys? Clancy darlin', they're not a whole lot younger than we are. Granted we've got a few years on 'em and a whole lot of livin' but don't go thinkin' 'bout motherin' 'em or adoptin' 'em, they're too old for that."

"Oh you, you know what I mean. They've had a rough time of it but that hasn't ruined 'em and I think they'll be a big help to us. Course none of us know much about cattle but those boys are smart and hard workin' and I'm glad we asked them to come."

"Me too, they learn fast and are willing to do whatever it takes to get the job done. I'm glad that Reuben's gonna come too. He's great with any kind of animals and he's excited about tryin' to catch some mustangs and breakin' 'em. You know babe," he contemplated as he looked at his partner, "I think this ranchin' things gonna be great for us, all of us." He received an affirmative smile in return as Clancy nodded her head and slipped back into planning mode.

The terrain flattened out into the broad expanse of grassland with occasional scattered rock formations and hidden ravines that provided minimal shelter for the animals of the plains. As the trail followed the low contours the rocking gait of the horses was disturbed by the clatter of hoofs on rocks or the dragging of a lazy foot by the pack-mule. An easy breeze aided the grasses as they waved at the passers-by and Caleb stood in his stirrups and pointed at a distant herd of antelope that stared back at the interruption to their grazing. Clancy stared at a large jack rabbit that sat on his haunches at the edge of the trail before them. With his foot-long ears held erect and his show-shoe feet giving stability to his stance, rabbit and woman stared at each other. Turning to her husband she said, "Those things amaze me, they've got ears the size of a mule and feet the size of a big man. Boy, God must've had a sense of humor when He made them!"

With a rolling chuckle Caleb answered, "Yeah, I suppose. But from what Pa says, there's plenty of things in this world that shows God has a sense of humor."

Standing in his stirrups, Caleb pointed and said, "Look yonder! That's Fort Bernard up thar! We made it with plenty of daylight left, guess you're gonna hafta put that turkey on a spit after all," as he smiled at his grinning wife. It was evident she was relieved to reach the fort. This would be where they would part from the brigade and strike off to the Medicine Bow and start their new home. Just the thought of it brought a special warm feeling to the woman and she smiled at her husband who wasn't thinking any further ahead than his next meal.

Fort Bernard sat along the North Platte with its palisade walls encompassing the home of the bourgeois Joseph Bissonette and the other structures for housing hides, peltries and trade goods. A low roofed log structure along the West palisade provided housing for the workers and a few spare bunks for others. Owned by the American Fur Company, the fort would be the re-supply point for the buffalo brigade. The mule train pulled alongside the North wall and the animals were loosed to graze in the nearby field. Caleb and Red visited with the trader John Richards at the trader's store and Caleb explained Red would be taking over the brigade and would need to re-supply now and perhaps again during or after their extended hunt. With arrangements made, Caleb left Red to dicker with the trader and returned to their camp by the trees along the bank of the North Platte. Clancy had already plucked the turkey and had it suspended on a strong green willow spit over the low burning fire. Reuben and the Threet brothers were watching as their mouths watered but looked up at the arrival of Caleb. "See there fellas, she's a mighty good cook and if we're not careful she'll fatten us up so much we won't be able to get any work done."

The three men smiled in appreciation and anticipation of the coming feast and the two boys squirmed on their seats. Caleb seated himself with them and began to share the plans for the coming days. "In the morning, we'll cut out a couple more mules and in the third wagon I've set aside some pack saddles and panniers and packs as well as the extra supplies I picked up in St. Louis. I've got a tool box and some other tools for building the cabins, and some other supplies as well. I'll be getting a few more supplies at the trader here, and with our mule and the two others, we should be able to handle it all. You fellas be sure to pick up all your belongings and if you need anything else, let me know and we'll see if the trader has what we need." As he sat quiet a moment considering the necessary preparations he looked at the three men and asked, "We, me and Clancy, want you to know we appreciate you comin' with us. I think we've got a good future for all of us, but it'll take a lot of work, and I want you to know, we'll share not only in the work but in the profits, if there are any, as well. Now, ya got any questions?"

Colton spoke up and asked, "This place we're goin', the Medicine Bow, does it look like this," he motioned to the flats of the prairie around them, "or are there mountains? We, Chance and I, were hopin' to see some mountains."

"Well, let me tell you. Believe it or not, this river right here," pointing at the North Platte, "makes a great big bend many miles North of here, then turns back South and the headwaters are in the mountains right near where we'll be makin' our home. The big difference though, is up there in the mountains the water flows fast, clear and sweet. We'll actually be between two different ranges of mountains, and we'll build our cabins overlooking the prettiest valley you ever did see and we can sit on the porch and look at the snowcapped peaks of the Medicine Bow as we drink our coffee." As Caleb finished his description he had a glassy stare that reflected the promise of their future. The three men sat still staring into the low burning cook fire and each one chased the pictures in their minds of what their new home would be like. Their reverie was broken by Clancy stirring the potpourri of wild vegetables in the hanging pot then lifted the lid of the Dutch oven to check on the biscuits. She pushed the coffee pot away from the flames to let the grounds settle and told the men, "Better get your plates and cups, dinner'll be ready in a jiffy."

With everyone taking to their assigned tasks, the gathering of supplies, packing of the mules, securing belongings and gear, the small cavalcade was ready to say their good byes. Red, Jesse, Don and several others gathered around and shook hands, wished good luck both ways, and patted backs and departed to their own tasks. The two old timers lingered a while longer and after shaking hands with Reuben and the boys, they tarried by Caleb and Clancy. When Clancy asked about their plans, Rooster said, "Wal, we'll be stickin' with these fellers fer a while, but we might heed the call of them thar mountains and hafta answer with a trip to that thar tall timber."

Caleb said, "I'd like to ask a favor of you fellas, if you're of a mind to. Our folks live with the Arapaho up in the Wind River mountains, and we'd be obliged if you get up thataway if you'd stop in and tell 'em you seen us and we're headin' to the Medicine Bow."

"Why shore, young'un. We was lookin' fer an excuse to head up thar, didn't you say they was som'eres near the Popo Agie?" asked Bones.

"Actually, their summer camp is usually up on the flats above the headwaters of the Popo Agie. It'd be pretty easy to find. We'd sure be grateful if you did."

Clancy added, "Do you really think you'd make it up there?" she asked excitedly.

"Wal, for you girl, we'd do just 'bout anything. You know we're shore gonna miss seein' yore purty face," then turning to Caleb, "not his so much, mind you, but we'll miss seein' you," said Rooster with his mischievous smile.

"O.K. then, I've got a very special message for you to deliver to our Ma and Pa, Laughing Waters and White Wolf or Jeremiah. She's the shaman of the village of Broken Shield."

"Why shore girl, whatchu want us to tell 'em?"

With a big grin and a glance at her husband she said, "Tell 'em they're gonna be grandparents come Spring and I'd sure like to have 'em there when it happens."

All three men, Rooster, Bones and Caleb looked like puppets on the same string as their heads snapped to look at Clancy with their mouths hanging open. When Caleb realized what she had said, he asked incredulously, "You're . . .you're . . . we're . . . we're gonna have a baby?"

She smiled broadly as she nodded her head and stifled a giggle as Caleb grabbed her in a bear hug and said, "Wow, . . .wow . . .that's great!

The two old timers hooked elbows and danced around in a circle laughing and said to Clancy, "So, we're gonna be Uncles are we?"

"Yes you are! Sometime late Spring, so you'll have to come see your new nephew!"

With hugs, handshakes and pats on the back, good-byes were said and the couple mounted up to join the waiting men. With waves and a few tears, they dug heels in the sides of the horses and started on the next chapter of this long adventure. Looking to the distance and searching for mountains, the cavalcade lined out pointed West.

THE LONG LEGGED APPALOOSAS SEEMED TO SENSE the mood change of their riders and stretched out their legs with their backs to the rising sun. With nothing but low rolling hills, sagebrush, cactus and buffalo grass before them and no distinct trail, the new found freedom lifted their heads higher, lengthened their stride and quickened their pace. The broad smiles on the couple's faces as they rode side by side revealed their excitement and anticipation of the new life that lay before them. Behind them, Reuben led their pack-mule and Colton and Chance, also riding side by side each trailed one of the newly chosen pack mules. The only member of the small troop that wasn't grinning was the usual stoic Reuben. But the sparkle in his eye told of his own hopes and dreams. Scarcely an hour passed and Reuben reined up and turned around and said, "Wait, do ya'll hear dat? Sumbuddy's a hollerin' back yonder! Dere it is agin."

Colton and Chance now turned around and

watching their back trail nodded and Chance quietly replied, "Yeah, I hear it."

In the distance a small dust cloud rose pushing a man on horseback yelling and waving a hat. The group had reined up and now watched the approaching figure that was coming at a full run as if something or someone was chasing him. "I don' see nobody else, must be sumpin' mighty wrong fer him to be a yellin' like dat," observed Reuben. He lifted his hand to shield his eyes from the sun behind the rider, stretched out a bit as if the extra few inches from his craning neck would give a better view and said, "Hah! That's that ragamuffin, Brewster! Now what's that boy up to?" As the horse slid to a stop beside the group, the boy hollered breathlessly, "Mr. Thompsett suh, I wanna go wid y'alls. When you asked me to join up with the brigade, I thought you meant you wanted me to ride all the way with you and here you done took off widout me. That ain't right! Cain't I go wit' you? You're da closest thing to a family I got." Stopping to take a breath of the dusty air, he looked at Caleb and Clancy with a hang dog look and pleaded with his eyes. Clancy cocked her head to one side, reached over and touched Caleb on the elbow so he would look at her and seeing her sympathetic motherly look knew he had no recourse. Turning to the boy he said, "Did you settle up with Red for that horse and tack you're on?"

"Oh yessir, he said what little wages I had comin' would cover it, and he even gave me five dollars for the rest! Can you believe it? I ain't never had nothin' before."

"Well, you're gonna work a lot harder than you have been and you're gonna earn a lot less if you come with us," snarled Caleb with an attempt to appear stern but failing.

"That's O.K., you don't even have to pay me, just let me tag along an' I'll be happy with that," promised the youngster. His face showed his youth but he was nearing the size of a man and the work on the trail had helped him to fill out his tattered shirt and breeches. The tanned skin under his dirty blonde hair and his broad shoulders resembled the Threet brothers and the boy could pass as a third brother.

"How old are you, anyway?" asked Caleb.

"Uh . . .I don't rightly know, I never knowed when my birthday was but I'm thinkin' I'm comin' on fifteen or so."

Caleb looked at Reuben seeking his approval since the boy had worked under the boss of the animals for the entire trip and if anyone knew his worth it would be Reuben. The smile and nod of the big man's head told him all he needed to know and Caleb turned to Brewster and said, "All right, come on along. One more mouth to feed won't make that much difference."

The first day out from the fort saw the adventurers make good time and cover most of thirty miles before they sought refuge at a grassy clearing in a copse of cottonwood by the riverbank. They were following the South bank of the Laramie River and would have ample water and graze for the animals and it looked like a restful place for their first night away from the noise and pandemonium of the mule train. Brewster pitched in as cook's helper and chattered incessantly seeking to learn all about campfire cooking as the ever patient Clancy smiled and quietly answered all his questions while giving him helpful instructions and guidance. Clancy fondly remembered the times when traveling with her Mum and Da that her mother would fix the meals for her family and most of the men that were without families. It was a common thing to have as many as ten people around their campfire and Clancy learned to fix meals that would be both tasty and filling even when the supplies were scarce.

Three more days' travel brought them to the foot of Elk Mountain, the lone sentinel at the Northernmost point of the Medicine Bow mountain range. The no name stream that meandered from the mountains ran cool and clear as it chuckled over the rocks and invited the travelers to stop and rest. After unpacking and picketing the animals Caleb directed Colton and Chance to scout around and try for a deer or other fresh meat. "Those two antelope we been dining on for the past few days are pretty slim pickings and a haunch of deer would be pretty tasty," he suggested. They agreed and happily started out on their first solo hunt. Clancy was working with some dough and had flour up to her elbows when she said, "A porch!" Then realizing she spoke out loud, she cast a sheepish grin at her husband who was looking at her with a question on his face. "A porch, I want a front porch on our home. One where we can sit and watch the sun come up or just watch the cattle or elk or whatever in the valley below us. I want a porch!"

"Uh, sure, I guess. Whatever my wife wants, she gets!" he proclaimed with a broad smile. Clancy looked at him, wiped away a dangling ringlet of red hair with the back of her hand leaving a trail of flour across her freckles and smiled a "Thank you."

As Clancy watched, Brewster pulled aside some coals from the fire, sat the Dutch oven on them and with their short handled shovel put more coals on the top and turned to Clancy for approval. She smiled at her protégé and turned at the hail of the returning brothers. Hanging on a long pole suspended from their shoulders was a sizable mule deer doe with its head dangling and chest open to the cool mountain breeze. The sight of fresh venison brought nods of approval from both Caleb and Clancy but as the brothers lowered their take to the ground, Colton looked at Caleb and said, "Uh, we found somethin' you might wanna take a look at."

Standing on a slight promontory that afforded a view of the far reaching plains to the North and East, Caleb rested his hands on his hips and tried to reconstruct the story of the tragedy that lay behind him. The remains of six prairie schooners were scattered on both sides of a slight draw that provided little protection. Some were partially burnt, others just broken down and pieces scattered. Bits of gingham clothes, now nothing but tattered rags, told of both men and women dying here and maybe children as well. As Chance neared his side, the young man asked, "So, what do you think happened here?"

"Well, as near as I can figger, it looks like some folks tried to make their own trail West and thought going South of the Oregon Trail might be easier. Others have tried it and weren't any luckier than these folks. From the looks of things, they thought they could make it over that saddle behind us and got stopped by the thick timber.

Maybe some Indians were after 'em, Cheyenne probably, and they made a stand of it here. I found a broken shaft of an arrow over yonder and a broken lance point that says it was a pretty good fight. I think the coyotes, wolves and buzzards did the rest. It's a shame that some folks think they know better and try to beat this country instead of workin' with it. This wild country is a grand place to live but if you don't know what you're doin' and don't learn from those that came before you, it'll beat you down every time." He turned and surveyed the scene of carnage again, shook his head and waved the others to come with him back to camp.

The somber group ate in silence until Reuben spoke up and asked, "Mr. Caleb," and was interrupted by Caleb with, "It's not Mr. Caleb, Reuben, just Caleb." The big man smiled and continued, "Yassuh, Caleb. I couldn't help but hear Ms. Clancy when she done tol' you she wants a po'ch, and I was thinkin' a po'ch takes boa'ds. And you ain't got no boa'ds, but dez lots a boa'ds back there in them wagons. How fah we gots ta go to where we gonna build them cabins?"

"Not more'n two days, as I calculate it," answered Caleb.

"Yassuh, wal da way I figguh it, if'n we put togethuh some o' dem runnin' gear, we could make us enuff of a wagon to haul most o' dat lumbuh them wagons has and it'd sho make a nice po'ch fo' Ms. Clancy. Mebbe even 'nuff fo a flo'" Clancy looked up with a new sparkle in her eyes as she looked first at Reuben then at Caleb and back at Reuben. Caleb saw her look and knew once again, there was no rhyme or reason that would convince her otherwise.

"Well, that's a pretty good idea Reuben. Do you think you could do that, with some help of course?"

"Yassuh, I do. Da only ting is, how fah is it to our new home and when do we staht buildin'?"

Caleb smiled at the 'new home' reference and replied, "I think we all need to get to our new home, make some temporary shelters for us and the animals, and then we'll plan out what we're gonna do. But I like what you're sayin' Reuben and the wood from those wagons would be a big help in building our new homes."

The thoughts, plans, hopes and dreams of the wanderers were as varied as the figures that lay wrapped in their bedrolls, but all focused on the one thought, 'our new homes' as they drifted off to sleep and dream. The stars danced overhead and peeked through the tall pine boughs to comfort the slumbering travelers and give promise of greater dreams in their near future.

WITH MEDICINE PEAK OFF THEIR LEFT SHOULDER, Elk Mountain behind them and following the shoulder of the Medicine Bow Range, the single file column of explorers savored the first sight of the spreading valley below them. Although framed by the rising bluffs and rim rock, the bottomland of the headwaters of the North Platte shone green and promising in the mid-day light. Expecting this last leg of their journey to take longer, they were pleasantly surprised and sat and gazed at the winding river and its accompanying green grasses and trees.

As they watched, several big eared mule deer raised their heads from their graze to examine the visitors and in the distance the growing family watched two young bull elk sparring before the on looking herd of cow elk. The clear waters of the North Platte did little to resemble the muddy and wide spreading stream along the Emigrant trail. Caleb dropped to the ground, motioned for Clancy to join him and waited as the rest also dismounted. With

Clancy by his side, he nodded to the promising valley and asked, "Now just where do you think you might want to build your new home?"

She let her eyes survey the stretch of the valley before them and asked, "Does it continue upstream?"

"Yes, but there's something you might want to consider," and he pointed to a wide spot in the river where a bend revealed a broad sand bar, "Just yonder by the river there are some hot springs. The Cheyenne, Ute and Southern Arapaho consider these to be magic waters and good for what ails ya."

She looked at Caleb to see if he was serious or kidding her and with his sober expression before her she said, "Really? Why didn't you say something about this before?"

"Well, I hadn't really thought about it until just now when I saw that steam hanging down there 'mongst those trees."

She continued to look over the terrain and spotting an arm of green that stretched up the far hillside, she shaded her eyes and looked for a spell. When Caleb and the others realized this might take a while, they found seats either on nearby stones or pushed aside some cactus and sat on the rocky ground. Finally, after examining the entire valley as best she could from this vantage point, she said, "Yeah, that looks like just the place. We can build the cabin back in the trees a ways and still be reasonably close to the water and be facing the rising sun. I think that'll do fine. But we need to look closer, of course." Without comment, the men mounted up and Caleb dug his heels into the ribs of his appaloosa to lead the cavalcade down the hillside trail toward their new home site.

As they crossed the river, they startled a pair of mule deer bucks that scampered a short distance, stopped and looked back at the rude intruders that chased them from their drink. Clancy led the way as she gigged her appaloosa to a trot, she was anxious to see the home site. With trees standing tall at the edge of the meadow, the spruce and pine painted a path up the narrow defile and rose to the higher reaches of the mountains behind. At the bottom of the draw was a narrow spring-fed creek that was an added and unexpected feature of her choice. Passing the sentinel trees at the edge of the clearing, a narrow game trail wound through the trees to a slight shoulder of ground that opened like a small park with thick grasses stretching to reach the bright rays of the mid-day sun. She smiled, dropped from the saddle, let Rowdy down to run and explore, ground tied her mount and walked the perimeter of the clearing. As she walked, she envisioned the cabin and as Caleb and company arrived, she said, "I want it right there," as she pointed then turned to face toward the valley, "See, through those trees we can see almost the entire valley and we'll see the sun come up right there at the shoulder of Medicine Peak!" she exclaimed excitedly. Caleb and Reuben and the three boys stood looking around and smiling then Reuben pointed at the uphill side of the clearing at another shoulder with a thin barrier of trees separating it from where they stood and said, "An that'd be a good spot fer a cabin fer us'ns and a shed fer da animals."

With all in agreement, they unpacked the mules,

removed the saddles and other tack from the horses, picketed all the animals and began to set to the work of temporary shelters for man and beast alike. Willing hands and eager hearts made short work of the immediate need for shelters and camp. The boys busied themselves gathering firewood, Reuben tended to the animals, leading them down into the meadow and hobbled them to ensure they wouldn't graze too far, and Caleb helped Clancy set up camp with the cook fire and bedrolls and more. It was a pleasant evening and the chatter around the fire was plentiful and all lingered longer than usual. Caleb cautioned everyone to always be vigilant because it would not be surprising to see any number of Indians. "The Cheyenne, Southern Arapaho, and Ute are pretty common around here. Now I think the Cheyenne and Arapaho we can get along with, what with our history with them, but I'm not too sure about the Ute. I've heard things both ways about them being friendly and warlike and this is more in their territory, so just be careful and don't start anything."

With that caution, everyone turned in for the night and as darkness overtook the travelers, all wore smiles into their slumber.

As the rising sun crested the shoulder of the distant Medicine Peak, Caleb and Clancy stood at the edge of the clearing arm in arm and watched as the underbellies of the clouds were painted with brilliant splashes of orange and gold. They looked at one another and embraced and Caleb said, "I don't know if this is Sunday or not, but I'm thinkin' we need to do somethin', could you roust out the fellas and have 'em come here?"

With a nod and a shrug of her shoulders as she wondered what her husband was up to, she went to the cook fire where the four were already seated and enjoying a morning cup of coffee. She motioned to them to follow her and returned to her husband's side. While she was gone he had taken his father's bible from his saddle bags and turned to watch them approach. As they gathered near he started, "Well, family, and that's what we are now, family, I'm not sure if this is Sunday or not, but I think there's somethin' we should do and that's what this is all about. My Pa taught that we should always be thankful and especially thankful to God for what he has given us," he looked at the open bible cradled in his hands and read, *"'Be careful for nothing, but in everything by prayer and supplication with thanksgiving, let your requests be made known unto God. And the peace of God, which passeth all understanding, shall keep your hearts and minds through Christ Jesus.'*

See, I believe we need to thank God for all He's done for us, bringing us safely this far and giving us this place. We, Clancy and me, have been prayin' 'bout this for some time now, and here we are. Now He, God, also says He'll give us peace and that's what we want is to live here in peace. So, I'm gonna say a little prayer if you'll just bow your heads." His simple prayer of thanksgiving and asking for a life of peace touched the hearts of each one and stirred the memories of the Threet boys of their parents that taught them from the Bible and encouraged them to come to know Christ as their Savior. Now they smiled, knowing they had been brought to this very place with this couple because of answered prayer.

With the amens said, they began discussing the work before them and duties were divided. Reuben would take Brewster and the necessary tools and return to the wagons and try to salvage as much as possible. The brothers would work with Caleb felling and trimming trees and bringing them to the clearing and Clancy would lay out the plans and tend to the animals. With all the men busy with the heavy work, it also fell to Clancy to do some hunting and providing the camp with meat. Although Caleb did down a nice young bull elk when they were on a scout for trees, she also brought in a couple of deer. She surprised the men for one evening meal with a nice batch of fried trout and the men never complained about her cooking, but rather heaped praise on her so much she had to shush them, but she enjoyed their praise and banter. She enjoyed being the mother of such a fine family of hard workers.

At the end of the first week, the clearing was cluttered with a good stockpile of logs, the stack of wagon lumber and the idle running gear used to transport the lumber. The horses and mules, when not in use which was often, became comfortable with the belly deep grass in the meadow and would never stray far from home. The men were anxious to begin the building and to see some progress on the cabins. With work assigned, the crew busied themselves shaping logs, gathering and laying stones for the foundation, and the many other tasks of building. Just over two weeks saw the completion of the main cabin and work begun on the second. Another two weeks, lots of calluses replacing blisters, countless splinters and sore muscles beyond measure and the two cabins were complete. Caleb and Clancy sat on the edge of their porch, since the making of furniture hadn't started, and watched as the tired men trudged toward their perch. As they seated themselves alongside the two, Chance was the first to speak as he said, "Finished, finally! Now we can sleep inside too!"

Clancy and Caleb laughed at the touch of jealousy from the young man and nodded at the weary men. For they were all men now, young and old alike, the brothers, Brewster and Reuben had become a team of hard working men and both Clancy and Caleb were proud of each and every one. Clancy thought, *my family, what good men they are and they make me so proud.*

Looking at the tired crew Caleb said, "How 'bout tomorrow we take the day off and go soak in the hot springs down yonder. I think it'd be good for some sore muscles, don't you?" Two men on either side of the couple leaned over and smiled at Caleb and nodded weary heads.

Soaking in hot spring mineral waters can be relieving and refreshing but also tiring. The time of allowing tired bodies to relax and enjoy the mineral massage was appreciated by all and now as they trudged back up the slight rise and through the trees to the cabins, Caleb reminded them of all the work remaining. "We still need to build a lean-to shelter for the animals, a corral for 'em, and a tack shed for the gear and tools. Then we need to stock up with firewood and lay in a store of meat for the winter and cut some grass for the animals, and then . . . " and he was hooted down by the workers and Clancy with a smattering of "We know, we know, there's lots of work. Always will be, just let us enjoy our day off!" He smiled and draped an arm around his red head's shoulder and drew her close as they walked the last few steps to their cabin. The men turned to the trail to their cabin and the couple seated themselves on the porch.

Clancy lay her head on her husband's shoulder, put her palm on her stomach and said, "I hope it's a boy, don't you?" While she rubbed the head of the dog, Rowdy, it took Caleb a while to change his line of thought and realized she was speaking of the baby. He drew her closer to his side, lay his cheek on her head and whispered, "Whatever God wants us to have, is fine with me." She grasped his knee and squeezed as she said, "And I want us to name him Caleb Jeremiah," smiling up at her husband. Gazing at the view of the Medicine Bow Mountains with a fresh dusting of early fall snow and the Aspen starting to show gold, he said, "It sure is great to be home, and this is gonna be a great place to raise a family, boys and girls alike. And they're probably all gonna have red hair and freckles!"

She pushed against him playfully and said, "Yup, ain't we lucky?"

The end, or not.

He had been challenged to carve a ranch out of the wilderness of the West. To partner with the brother of one of the most successful ranchers in Texas and build the first ranch in the wilds of the territories. Caleb and his wife and friends chose to confront the wilds of what would become Wyoming territory and establish one of the first ranches in that desolate country. Little did it matter that they knew nothing about ranching or cattle but the challenge had been given and accepted. However, the land he chose lay between the Ute Indians and their enemy, the Cheyenne and with all the other difficulties that included an unmerciful winter, a pack of hungry wolves, and a monster mama grizzly bear bent on protecting her cubs, what more could be thrown their way?

Gunfights, Indian Wars, nature's fury, and more assault the pioneers as they seek to build the first cattle ranch along the Cherokee Trail. Yet the new frontier fought back against anyone that sought to leave their mark on the virgin territory claimed by the wild animals and the Native Americans. But destiny would have a hand and that hand had been dealt. What would be the outcome of this game of life?

AVAILABLE NOW FROM B.N. RUNDELL AND WOLFPACK PUBLISHING

Born and raised in Colorado into a family of ranchers and cowboys, B.N. is the youngest of seven sons. Juggling bull riding, skiing, and high school, graduation was a launching pad for a hitch in the Army Paratroopers. After the army, he finished his college education in Springfield, MO, and together with his wife and growing family, entered the ministry as a Baptist preacher.

Together, B.N. and Dawn raised four girls that are now married and have made them proud grandparents. With many years as a successful pastor and educator, he retired from the ministry and followed in the footsteps of his entrepreneurial father and started a successful insurance agency, which is now in the hands of his trusted nephew. He has also been a successful audiobook narrator and has recorded many books for several award-winning authors. Now finally realizing his life-long dream, B.N. has turned his efforts to writing a variety of books, from children's picture books and young adult adventure books, to the historical fiction and western genres which are his first love.